"How did you know my name?" she demanded.

He stood, forcing himself to relax, or at least to look as if he didn't have all these turbulent emotions fighting it out in his gut. "Hello, Abby," he said softly. "I'm Michael Dance."

"I don't know a Michael Dance," she said.

"No, you probably don't remember me. It's been a while. Five years."

She searched his face, panic behind her eyes. He wanted to reach out, to reassure her. But he remained frozen, immobile. "You knew me in Afghanistan?" she asked. "I don't remember."

"There's no reason you should," he said. "The last time I saw you, you were pretty out of it. Technically, you were dead—for a while, at least."

He'd been the one to bring her back to life, massaging her heart and breathing into her ravaged mouth until her heart beat again and she sucked in oxygen on her own. He'd saved her life, and in that moment forged a connection he'd never been quite able to sever.

THE GUARDIAN

CINDI MYERS

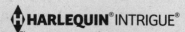

For Katie

Recycling programs
for this product may
not exist in your area.

ISBN-13: 978-0-373-69839-4

The Guardian

Copyright © 2015 by Cynthia Myers

This edition published by arrangement with Harlequin Books S.A.

For questions and comments about the quality of this book, please contact us at CustomerService@Harlequin.com.

® and TM are trademarks of Harlequin Enterprises Limited or its corporate affiliates. Trademarks indicated with ® are registered in the United States Patent and Trademark Office, the Canadian Intellectual Property Office and in other countries.

Printed in U.S.A.

www.Harlequin.com

Cindi Myers is an author of more than fifty novels. When she's not crafting new romance plots, she enjoys skiing, gardening, cooking, crafting and daydreaming. A lover of small-town life, she lives with her husband and two spoiled dogs in the Colorado mountains.

Books by Cindi Myers

The Ranger Brigade series

The Guardian

HARLEQUIN INTRIGUE

Rocky Mountain Revenge
Rocky Mountain Rescue

HARLEQUIN HEARTWARMING

Her Cowboy Soldier
What She'd Do for Love

Visit the Author Profile page at Harlequin.com for more titles.

CAST OF CHARACTERS

Abby Stewart—The former beauty queen suffered a devastating injury while serving in Afghanistan. Now a graduate student studying rare plants, she finds peace in the backcountry of Black Canyon of the Gunnison National Park. But even this remote location isn't immune from violence.

Lieutenant Michael Dance—In Afghanistan, he saved lives as part of the elite air force pararescuemen (PJs). Now he's a border patrol agent assigned to a task force charged with fighting crime on national park lands.

Captain Graham Ellison—The FBI agent heads up the task force known as The Ranger Brigade. A former marine, Ellison must battle both criminals on public lands and the politicians and press who think the task force is a waste of money.

Richard Prentice—The billionaire owns property on the park boundaries and has made a career of thumbing his nose at the federal government. Does he try to thwart the Rangers' efforts on principle, or does he have something to hide?

Raul Meredes—A criminal with ties to Mexican drug cartels, Meredes oversees a drug and human smuggling operation within the National Park.

Mariposa—The beautiful Mexican immigrant makes friends with Abby, but is she a victim of Meredes, or his coconspirator?

Lauren Starling—The beautiful news reporter has a history of erratic behavior. She's been reported missing and was last seen in the National Park.

Lieutenant Randall Knightbridge—The BLM agent is the youngest member of the task force and investigates with the help of Lotte, his Belgian Malinois.

Carmen Redhorse—The only female member of the task force works for the Colorado Bureau of Investigation.

Marco Cruz—The DEA agent is former Special Forces and the task force's best tracker.

Simon Woolridge—The acerbic ICE officer is the task force's computer whiz, but he and Michael don't see eye to eye on the treatment of illegal immigrants.

Lance Carpenter—The Montrose County sheriff's deputy is the task force's liaison with local law enforcement.

Chapter One

Abby Stewart was not lost. Maybe she'd wandered a little off her planned route, but she wasn't lost.

She was a scientist and a decorated war veteran. She had GPS and maps and a good sense of direction. So she couldn't be lost. But standing in the middle of nowhere in the Colorado wilderness did have her a little disoriented, she could admit. The problem was, the terrain around Black Canyon of the Gunnison National Park tended to all look the same after a while: thousands of acres of rugged, roadless wilderness covered in piñon forests, and scrubby desert set against a backdrop of spectacular mountain views. People did get lost out here every year.

But Abby wasn't one of them, she reminded herself again. She took a deep breath and consulted her handheld GPS. There was the shallow draw she'd just passed, and to the west were the foothills of the Cimarron Mountains. And there was her location now. The display showed she'd hiked three miles from her car. All she had to do was head northeast and she'd eventually make it back to her parking spot and the red dirt two-track she'd driven in on. Feeling more reassured, she returned the GPS unit to her backpack and scanned the landscape around her. To a casual observer, the place probably looked pretty desolate—a high plateau of scrubby grass, cactus and stunted juniper. But to Abby, who was on her way to earning a master's degree in environmental science, the Black Canyon of the Gunnison was a treasure trove of more than eight hundred plant species, including the handful she was focusing on in her research.

Her anxiety over temporarily losing her bearings vanished as she focused on a gray-green clump of vegetation in the shadow of a misshapen piñon. She bent over, peering closer, and a surge of triumph filled her. *Yes!* A terrific specimen of *Lomatium concinnum*— desert parsley to the layman. Number four on the list of species she needed to collect for her research. She knelt and slipped off her pack and quickly took out a digital camera, small trowel and collecting bag.

Intent on photographing the parsley in place, then carefully digging it up, leaving as much of the root system intact as possible, she missed the sounds of approaching footsteps until they were almost on her. A branch crackled and she started, heart pounding. She peered into the dense underbrush in front of her, in the direction of the sound, and heard a shuffling noise— the muffled swish of fabric rubbing against the brush. Whoever this was wasn't trying to be particularly quiet, but what were they doing out here, literally in the middle of nowhere?

In the week Abby had been camped in the area she'd seen fewer than a dozen other people since checking in at the park ranger station, and all of those had been in the campground or along the paved road. Here in the backcountry she'd imagined herself completely alone.

Stealthily, she slid the Sig Sauer from the holster at her side. She'd told the few friends who'd asked about the gun that she carried it to deal with snakes and other wildlife she might encounter in the backcountry, but the truth was, ever since her stint in Afghanistan, she felt safer armed when she went out alone. Flashes of unsettling memories crowded her mind as she drew the weapon; suddenly, she was back in Kandahar, stalking insurgents who'd just wiped out half her patrol group. As a woman, she'd often been tasked with going into the homes of locals to question the women there with the aid of an interpreter. Every time she stepped into one of those homes, she wondered if she'd come out alive. This scene had the same sense of being cut off from the rest of the world, the same sense of paranoia and danger.

Heart racing, she struggled to control her breathing and to push the memories away. She wasn't in Afghanistan. She was in Colorado. In a national park. She was safe. This was probably just another hiker, someone else who appreciated the solitude and peace of the wilderness. She inched forward and pushed aside the feathery, aromatic branches of a piñon.

A small, dark woman bent over the ground, deftly pulling up plants and stuffing them into the pockets of her full skirt. Dandelions, Abby noted. A popular edible wild green. She replaced the gun in its holster and stood. "Hello," she said.

The woman jumped and dropped a handful of dandelions. She turned, as if to run. "Wait!" Abby called. "I'm sorry. I didn't mean to frighten you." She retrieved the plants and held them out to the woman. She was young, barely out of her teens, and very beautiful. Her skin was the rich brown of toffee, and she had high cheekbones, a rosebud mouth and large black eyes framed by lacy lashes. She wore a loose blue blouse, a long, full skirt and leather sandals, with a plaid shawl draped across her body.

She came forward and hesitantly accepted the dandelions from Abby. *"Gracias,"* she said, her voice just above a whisper.

Latina, Abby thought. A large community of Mexican immigrants lived in the area. She searched her mind for what schoolgirl Spanish she could recall. *"Habla inglés?"*

The woman shook her head and wrapped her arms around what Abby had first assumed to be a bag for storing the plants she collected, but she now realized was a swaddled infant, cradled close to the woman's torso with a sling made from the red, blue and green shawl. "You have a baby!" Abby smiled. "A *niño*," she added.

The woman held the baby closer and stared at Abby, eyes wide with fear.

Maybe she was an illegal, afraid Abby would report her to the authorities. "Don't worry," Abby said, unable to remember the Spanish words. "I'm looking for plants, like you." She broke a stem from the desert parsley and held it out. *"Donde esta este?"* she asked. *Where is this?*

The woman eyed Abby warily, but stepped forward to study the plant. She nodded. *"Si. Yo conozco."*

"You know this plant? Can you show me where to find more? *Donde esta*?"

The woman looked around, then motioned Abby to follow her. Abby did so, excitement growing. So far, specimens of *Lomatium* had been rare. Having more plants to study would be a tremendous find.

The woman moved rapidly over the rough ground despite her long skirts and the burden of the baby. Her black hair swung behind her in a ponytail that reached almost to her waist. Where did she live? The closest homes were miles from here, and the only road into this section of the park was the one Abby had come in on. Was she collecting the dandelions because she had an interest in wild food—or because it was the only thing she had to eat?

The woman stopped abruptly beside a large rock and looked down at the ground. Desert parsley spread out for several feet in every direction—the most specimens Abby had ever seen. Her smile widened. "That's wonderful. Thank you so much. *Muchas gracias*." She clasped the woman's hand and shook it. The woman offered a shy smile.

"*Mi nombre es* Abby."

"*Soy* Mariposa," the woman said.

Mariposa. Butterfly. Her name was butterfly? "*Y su niño?*" Abby nodded to the baby.

Mariposa smiled and folded back the blanket to reveal a tiny dark-haired infant. "*Es una niña,*" she said. "Angelique."

"Angelique," Abby repeated. A little angel.

"*Usted ha cido harido.*" Mariposa lightly touched the side of Abby's face.

Abby flinched. Not because the touch was painful, but because she didn't like being reminded of the scar there. Multiple surgeries and time had faded the wound made by shrapnel from a roadside bomb, but the puckered white gash that ran from just above her left ear to midcheekbone would never be entirely gone. She wore her hair long and brushed forward to hide the worst of the scar, but alone in the wilderness on this warm day she'd clipped her hair back to keep it out of the way while she worked. She had no idea what the Spanish words Mariposa had spoken meant, but she was sure they were in reference to this disfigurement. *"Es no importante,"* she said, shaking her head.

She turned away, the profile of her good side to the woman, and spotted a delicate white flower. The three round petals blushed a deep purplish pink near their center. Half a dozen similar blooms rose nearby on slender, leafless stems. Abby knelt and slipped off her backpack and took out her trowel. She deftly dug up one of the flowers, revealing a fat white bulb. She brushed the dirt from the bulb and handed the plant to the woman. *"Este es comer. Bueno."* Her paltry Spanish frustrated her. "It's good to eat," she said, as if the English would make any more sense to her new friend.

Mariposa stroked the velvety petal of the flower and nodded. "It's called a mariposa lily," Abby said. *"Su nombre es Mariposa tambien."*

Mariposa nodded, then knelt and began digging up a second lily. Maybe she was just humoring Abby—or maybe she really needed the food. Abby hoped it was the former. As much as her studies had taught her about wild plants, she'd hate to have to depend on them for survival.

She turned to her pack once more and took out another collection bag, then remembered the energy bars stashed on the opposite side of the pack. They weren't much, but she'd give them to Mariposa. They'd at least be a change from roots. She found three bars and pressed them into the woman's hands. *"Por usted,"* she said.

"Gracias." Mariposa slipped the bars into the pocket of her skirt, then watched as Abby took out the camera and photographed the parsley plants. On impulse, she turned and aimed the camera at Mariposa. *Click.* And there she was, captured on the screen of the camera, face solemn but still very beautiful.

"You don't mind, do you?" Abby asked. She turned the camera so that the woman could see the picture.

Mariposa squinted at the image, but said nothing.

For a few minutes, the two women worked side by side, Mariposa digging lilies and Abby collecting more specimens of parsley. Though Abby usually preferred to work alone, it was nice being with Mariposa. She only wished she spoke better Spanish or Mariposa knew English, so she could find out more about where her new friend was from and why she was here in such a remote location.

Though the army had trained Abby to always be attuned to changes in the landscape around her, she must have gotten rusty since her return to civilian life. Mariposa was the first to stiffen and look toward the brush to the right of the women.

Abby heard the movements a second later—a group of people moving through the brush toward them, their voices carrying in the still air, though they were still some distance away.

She was about to ask Mariposa if she knew these newcomers when the young woman took off running. Her sudden departure startled Abby so much she didn't immediately react. She stared after the young woman, trying to make sense of what she was seeing.

Mariposa ran with her skirt held up, legs lifted high, in the opposite direction of the approaching strangers, stumbling over the uneven terrain as if her life depended on it. Abby debated running after her, but what would that do but frighten the woman more? She watched the fleeing figure until she'd disappeared over a slight rise, then glanced back toward the voices. They were getting louder, moving closer at a rapid pace.

Abby slipped on the pack and unholstered the weapon once more, then settled into the shade of a boulder to wait.

The group moved steadily toward her. All men, from the sound of them. The uneven terrain and stubby trees blocked them from view, but their voices carried easily in the stillness. They weren't attempting stealth; instead, they shouted and crashed through the underbrush with a great crackling of breaking twigs and branches. As they neared she thought she heard both English and Spanish. They seemed to be searching for someone, shouting, "Come out!" and, "Where is he?"

Or were they saying, "Where is *she*?" Were they looking for Mariposa? Why?

The first gunshots sent a jolt of adrenaline to her heart. She gripped the pistol more tightly and hunkered down closer to the boulder. For a moment she was back in Afghanistan, pinned down by enemy fire, unable to fight back. She closed her eyes and clenched her teeth, fighting for calm. She wasn't over there anymore. She was in the United States. No one was shooting at her. She was safe.

A second rapid burst of gunfire shattered the air, and Abby bit down on her lip so hard she tasted blood. Then everything went still. The echo of the concussion reverberated in the air, ringing in her ears. She couldn't hear the men anymore, though whether because they were silent or because she was momentarily deaf, she didn't know. She opened her eyes and reached into the pocket of her jeans to grip the small ceramic figure of a rabbit she kept there. She'd awoken in the field hospital with it clutched in her hand; she had no idea who had put the rabbit there, but ever since, she'd kept it as a kind of good-luck charm. The familiar feel of its smooth sides and little pointed ears calmed her. She was safe. She was all right.

The voices drifted to her once more, less agitated now, and receding. They gradually faded altogether, until everything around her was silent once more.

She waited a full ten minutes behind the boulder, clutching the pistol in both hands, every muscle tensed and poised to defend herself. After the clock on her phone told her the time she'd allotted had passed, she stood and scanned the wilderness around her. Nothing. No men, no Mariposa, no dust clouds marking the trail of a vehicle. The landscape was as still as a painting, not even a breeze stirring the leaves of the stunted trees.

Still shaky from the adrenaline rush, she holstered the pistol and settled the backpack more firmly on her shoulder. She could return to her car, but would that increase her chances of running into the men? Maybe it would be better to remain here for a while longer. She'd go about her business and give the men time to move farther away.

She returned to the parsley plants. Digging up the specimen calmed her further. She cradled the uprooted plant in her fingers and slid it into the plastic collection bag, then labeled the bag with the date, time and GPS coordinates where she'd found it, and stowed it in her pack. Then she stood and stretched. Her muscles ached from tension. Time to head back to camp. She'd clean up, then stop by the ranger station and report the men and the shooting—but not Mariposa. She had no desire to betray the woman's secrets, whatever they were.

She checked her GPS to orient herself, then turned southwest, in the direction of her car and the road. She had no trail to follow, only paths made by animals and the red line on the GPS unit that marked her route into this area. On patrol in Kandahar she'd used similar GPS units, but just as often she'd relied on the memory of landmarks or even the positioning of stars. Nothing over there had ever felt familiar to her, but she'd learned to accept the unfamiliarity, until the day that roadside bomb had almost taken everything away.

She picked her way carefully through the rough landscape, around clumps of prickly pear cactus and desert willows, past sagebrush and Mormon tea and dozens of other plants she identified out of long habit. She kept her eyes focused down, hoping to spot one of the other coveted species on her list. All the plants were considered rare in the area, and all held promise of medical uses. The research she was doing now might one day lead to cultivation of these species to treat cancer or Parkinson's or some other crippling disease.

So focused was she on cataloging the plants around her that she didn't see the fallen branch until she'd stumbled over it. Cursing her own clumsiness, she straightened and looked back at the offending obstacle. It stuck out from beneath a clump of rabbitbrush, dark brown and as big around as a man's arm. What kind of a tree would that be, the bark such a dark color—and out here in an area where large trees were rare?

She bent to look closer and cold horror swept over

her. She hadn't fallen over a branch at all. The thing that had tripped her was a man. He lay sprawled on the ground, arms outstretched, lifeless eyes staring up at her, long past seeing anything.

Chapter Two

Lieutenant Michael Dance had a low tolerance for meetings. As much as they were necessary to do his job, he endured them. But he'd wasted too many hours sitting in conference rooms, listening to other people drone on about things he didn't consider important. He preferred to be out in the field, doing real work that counted.

The person who'd called this meeting, however, was his boss, Captain Graham Ellison, aka "G-Man." Though Graham was with the FBI and Dance worked for Customs and Border Protection, Graham headed up the interagency task force charged with maintaining law and order on this vast swath of public land in southwest Colorado. And in their short acquaintance, Graham struck Michael as being someone worth listening to.

"National park rangers found an abandoned vehicle at the Dragon Point overlook yesterday," Graham said. A burly guy with the thick neck and wide shoulders of a linebacker and the short-cropped hair and erect stance of ex-military, Graham spoke softly, like many big men. His very presence commanded attention, so he didn't need to raise his voice. "The Montrose County sheriff's office has identified it as belonging to a Lauren Starling of Denver. Ms. Starling failed to show for work this morning, so they've asked us to keep an eye out. Here's a picture."

He passed around a glossy eight-by-ten photograph. Michael studied the studio head shot of a thirtysomething blonde with shoulder-length curls, violet-blue eyes and a dazzling white smile. She looked directly at the camera, beautiful and confident. "Do they think she was out here alone?" he asked, as he passed the photo on to the man next to him, Randall Knightbridge, with the Bureau of Land Management.

"They don't know," Graham said. "Right now they're just asking us to keep an eye out for her."

"Hey, I know this chick," Randall said.

Everyone turned to stare. The BLM ranger was the youngest member of the task force, in his late twenties and an acknowledged geek. He could rattle off the plots of half a dozen paranormal series on television, played lacrosse in his spare time and wore long-sleeved uniform shirts year-round to hide the colorful tattoos that decorated both arms. He didn't have a rep as a ladies' man, so what was he doing knowing a glamour girl like the one in the picture?

"I mean, I don't know her personally," he corrected, as if reading Michael's thoughts. "But I've seen her on TV. She does the news on channel nine in Denver."

"You're right." Simon Woolridge, with Immigration and Customs Enforcement, grabbed the picture and gave it a second look. "I knew she looked familiar."

"Like one of your ex-wives," quipped Lance Carpenter, a Montrose County sheriff's deputy.

"Lauren Starling is the evening news anchor for channel nine," Graham confirmed. "Her high profile is one reason this case is getting special attention from everyone involved."

"When did she go missing?" Marco Cruz, an agent with the DEA, asked.

"The Denver police aren't treating it as a missing person case yet," Graham said. "The car was simply parked at the overlook. There were no signs of a struggle. She took a week's vacation and didn't tell anyone where she was going. Nothing significant is missing from her apartment. That's all the information I have at the moment."

"Are they thinking suicide?" asked Carmen Redhorse, the only female member of the task force. Petite and dark haired, Carmen worked with the Colorado Bureau of Investigation.

No one looked surprised at her suggestion of suicide. Unfortunately, the deep canyon and steep drop-offs of Black Canyon of the Gunnison National Park were popular places for the despondent to end it all. Four or five people committed suicide in the park each year.

"There's no note," Graham said. "The Denver police are on the case right now. They've simply asked us to keep an eye on things. If you see anything suspicious, we'll pass it on to the local authorities." He consulted the clipboard in his hand. "On to more pressing matters. State police impounded a truck carrying a hundred pounds of fresh marijuana bud at a truck stop in Gunnison last night. The pot was concealed inside a load of coffee, but the drug dogs picked up the scent, no problem."

"When will these rubes learn they can't fool a dog's nose?" Randall leaned down to pet his Belgian Malinois, Lotte, who'd stretched out beneath his chair. She thumped the floor twice with her plume of a tail, but didn't raise her head.

"The logbook indicates the truck passed through this area," Graham continued. "That's the second shipment that's been waylaid in as many months, and another indication that there's an active growing operation in the area. We know from experience that public lands are prime targets for illegal growers."

"Free land, away from people, limited law enforcement presence." Carmen ticked off the reasons wilderness areas presented such a temptation to drug runners. "I read the first national parks had problems with bootleggers. Now it's pot and meth."

Graham turned to the large map of the area that covered most of one wall of the trailer that served as task force headquarters. "We're going to be flying more surveillance this week, trying to locate the growing fields. We'll be concentrating on the Gunnison Gorge just west of the park boundaries. The counters we laid last week show increased vehicle traffic on the roads in that area."

In addition to the more than thirty thousand acres within the national park, the task force was charged with controlling crime within the almost sixty-three thousand acres of the Gunnison Gorge National Conservation Area and the forty-three thousand acres of the Curecanti National Recreation Area. It was a ridiculous amount of land for a few people to patrol, much of it almost inaccessible, roadless wilderness. In recent years, drug cartels had taken advantage of short-staffed park service to cultivate thousands of acres of public land. They dug irrigation canals, built fences and destroyed priceless artifacts with impunity. This task force was an attempt to stop them.

A pretty feeble attempt, Michael thought. He thumbed a butterscotch Life Saver from the roll he kept in his pocket and popped it into his mouth. They were wasting time sitting around talking about the problem, instead of being out there doing something about it.

"If we want to find the crops, look for the people who take care of the crops," Simon said.

"You mean the people who plant the weed?" Randall asked.

"The people who plant it and water it and weed it and guard it from predators—both animal and human," Simon said. "Illegals, most likely, shipped in for that purpose. We find them and put pressure on them, we can find the person behind this. The money man."

Here was something Michael knew about. "Human trafficking in Colorado is up twenty percent this year," he said. "Some sources suggest a lot of victims who end up in Denver come from this area. We could be looking at a pipeline for more than drugs."

"So the guys in charge of drugs offer a free pass into the country to people who will work for them?" Lance asked.

"More likely they work with coyotes who charge people to bring them into the country, but instead of going to their cousin in Fort Collins or their aunt in Laramie, they end up prisoners of this drug cartel," Michael said. "And once they've worked the fields for a while or learned to cook up meth or whatever the drug lords need them to do, they take the women and the younger men to Denver and turn them out as prostitutes. It's slavery on a scale people have no idea even exists anymore."

"So in addition to drugs, we may be dealing with human trafficking," Carmen said.

"We don't know that." Simon's voice was dismissive. "It's only speculation. We do know that if these people have workers, they're probably illegals. Deport the workforce and you can cripple an operation. At least temporarily."

"Only until they bring in the next load of workers." Michael glared at the man across the conference table. "Rounding up people and deporting them solves nothing. And you miss the chance to break up the trafficking pipeline."

"End the drug operation and you remove the reason they have to bring in people," Simon countered.

"Right. And now they take them straight to Denver, where no one even notices what's going on."

"Back to the discussion at hand." Graham cut them off. He gave each of them a stern look. "As a task force, our job is to address all serious crime in this region, whether it's human trafficking or drugs or money laundering or murder. But I don't have to tell you that in this time of budget cuts, we have to be able to show the politicians are getting their money's worth. A high-profile case could do a lot to assure we all get to keep working."

And drugs were worth more to federal coffers than people, Michael thought grimly. The law allowed the Feds to seize any and all property involved in drug crimes, from cash and cars to mansions.

"Tomorrow we'll begin five days of aerial patrols, focused on these sectors." Graham indicated half a dozen spots on the map. "These are fairly level spots with access to water, remote, but possible to reach in four-wheel-drive vehicles."

"What about the private property in the area?" Michael asked. Several white spots on the map, some completely surrounded by federal land, indicated acreage owned by private individuals.

"Private property could provide an access point for the drug runners, so we'll be looking at that. Most of the private land is unoccupied," Graham said.

"Except for Prentice's fortress," Simon said.

Michael didn't ask the obvious question. If he waited, someone would explain this mystery to the new guy; if not, he'd find out what he needed to know on his own.

"Richard Prentice owns the land here." Graham pointed to a white square closest to the park—almost on the canyon rim. "He's built a compound there with several houses, stables, a gated entrance, et cetera."

"But before that, he tried to blackmail the government into buying the place at an exorbitant price," Carmen said. "He threatened to build this giant triple-X theater with huge neon signs practically at the park entrance." Her lip curled in disgust.

"He's had success with those kinds of tactics before," Graham said. "He threatened to blow up a historic building over near Ouray until a conservation group raised the money to buy the place from him."

"At an inflated price," Carmen said. "That's how he operates. If he can figure out a way to exploit a situation for money, he will."

"But the government didn't bite this time?" Michael asked.

"No," Lance said. "And the county fought back by passing an ordinance prohibiting sexually oriented businesses. He built a mansion instead, and spends his time filing harassment complaints every time we drive by or fly over."

"So do we think he has anything to do with the crime wave around here?" Michael asked. Greed and a lust for power were motivation enough for all manner of misdeeds.

Graham shook his head. "Prentice likes to thumb his nose at the government, but we have no reason to suspect he's guilty of any felonies."

"Which doesn't mean he isn't guilty," Carmen said. "Just that we can't prove it—yet."

Michael studied the map again. First chance he got, he'd check out this Prentice guy.

"Next on the list." Graham scanned the clipboard again, but before he could continue, a knock sounded on the door.

"Come in," Graham called.

The door opened and a woman stood on the threshold, eyes wide with surprise. A fall of long honey-blond hair obscured most of her face, but she appeared young, and pretty, with dark eyes and a well-shaped nose and chin. She wore canvas cargo pants, hiking boots and a long-sleeved canvas shirt, open at the throat to reveal a black tank top trimmed in lace, and a hint of tanned cleavage. Michael's gaze locked on the holstered weapon at her side—a .40-caliber Sig Sauer. He had one like it at his hip. So was she some kind of law enforcement? A new member of the team no one had mentioned?

"I, uh, I didn't mean to interrupt," she said. "I was looking for the park rangers. Their office was closed, and I saw the cars over here…"

"The park rangers go home at four," Graham said.

"They'll be in at nine in the morning if you need help with camping permits or something."

Her eyes narrowed, focused on the tan uniforms, then on the name badge pinned to Graham's shirt pocket. "Captain Ellison. Are you a law enforcement officer?"

"Yes. Can I help you?"

She pressed her lips together, as if debating her next move, then nodded. "I need to report a crime. A murder."

The temperature in the room dropped several degrees, Michael was sure, and the group around the table leaned forward, all eyes—including the dog's—focused on the petite woman in the doorway.

"Why don't you come in and give us a few more details." Graham motioned the woman forward.

As she moved past him, Michael caught the scents of wood smoke and sweat and something lighter and more feminine—a floral perfume or shampoo. An awareness stirred in his gut, a sense of familiarity, and the hair rose on the back of his neck. Where had he seen this woman before?

"I'm a biologist," she said, speaking primarily to Graham, but casting nervous glances at the rest of them. "Or rather, I'm working on my master's degree in biology. I'm studying several plant species found in the park for my thesis. I was out collecting specimens this morning when I heard people approaching. They were shouting in English and in Spanish, and they appeared to be searching for someone."

"Did you get close to them?" Simon asked. "Did you talk to them?"

She shook her head. As she did so, her hair swung

away from her face, revealing a jagged scar diagonally bisecting one cheek. The scar was bizarrely out of place on such a beautiful face, like a crack in an otherwise pristine china plate. Michael's gut tightened, and he struggled to control his breathing. He was sure he knew her now, but maybe his mind was playing tricks on him. Post-traumatic stress throwing up some new, bizarre symptom.

"They were some distance away—maybe two hundred yards," she continued. "I hid behind a large boulder and waited for them to leave."

"Why did you do that?" Simon asked.

"Because she's smart," Carmen said. "A woman alone in the middle of nowhere sees a group of rowdy men? Of course she hides."

Simon flushed, like a kid who's been reprimanded. "She looks as though she can take care of herself." He nodded to the weapon at her side. "You got a permit for that thing?"

"Yes." She turned away from him. "I couldn't see what they were doing—the terrain is rough out there. But I heard gunshots. Then they quieted down and left."

"You're sure they were gunshots?" Graham asked.

She nodded. "I was in the army, stationed in Kandahar. I know what gunfire sounds like. This was a semi-automatic. A rifle, not a handgun."

Michael gripped the underside of the conference table until his fingers ached. This was no trick of a war-stressed mind. This was *her*—the woman who'd lingered in the back of his mind for the better part of five years. The one he could never forget.

"All right." Graham leaned against the table, his pose deceptively casual. "What happened next?"

"I waited ten minutes to make sure they were gone, then I resumed collecting the specimens I'd come for. I headed back toward the road where I'd parked my car. I had walked less than half a mile when I stumbled over something." Her face paled and she swallowed hard, her lips pressed tightly together, holding in emotion. "It was a body," she said softly. Then, in a stronger voice, "A young man. Latino. He'd been shot in the chest."

"He was dead?" Randall asked.

"Oh, yes. But not for long. The body was still warm."

"So you think the men you heard shot him." Simon couldn't keep quiet long. Clearly, he liked playing the role of interrogator.

"It's your job to decide that, not mine," the woman said, a sharp edge to her voice. Good for her, Michael thought. Put Simon in his place.

"Can you show us where the body is?" Graham asked.

She nodded. "I think so. I was collecting specimens near there and I made note of the GPS coordinates. I should have noted the coordinates for the body, too, but seeing it out there was such a shock…" She looked down at the floor, hair falling forward to obscure her face once more. But Michael didn't need the visual confirmation anymore. This was *her*. And to think he'd thought he'd never see her again.

What were the odds that he'd run into her now—in this place half a world away from where they'd last met? Then again, his mother always said everything happened for a reason. Michael told himself he didn't believe in that kind of divine interference—in fate. But maybe some of his mother's superstition had rubbed off on him.

"We'll want a full statement from you later." Graham pulled out a pen and turned to a fresh sheet on his clipboard. "Right now, if you'll just give me your name and tell me where you're camped."

"Abigail Stewart."

Only when the others turned toward him did Michael realize he'd spoken out loud. Abby stared at him, too, her mouth half-open, a red stain coloring her previously pale cheeks. "How did you know my name?" she demanded.

He stood, forcing himself to relax, or at least to look as if he didn't have all these turbulent emotions fighting it out in his gut. "Hello, Abby," he said softly. "I'm Michael Dance."

"I don't know a Michael Dance," she said.

"No, you probably don't remember me. It's been a while. Five years."

She searched his face, panic behind her eyes. He wanted to reach out, to reassure her. But he remained frozen, immobile.

"You knew me in Afghanistan?" she asked. "I don't remember."

"There's no reason you should," he said. "The last time I saw you, you were pretty out of it. Technically, you were dead—for a while, at least."

He'd been the one to bring her back to life, massaging her heart and breathing in her ravaged mouth until her heart beat again and she'd sucked in oxygen on her own. He'd saved her life, and in that moment forged a connection he'd never been quite able to sever.

Chapter Three

Having a total stranger announce to a bunch of other strangers that you'd come back from the dead didn't rank high on Abby's list of experiences she wanted to repeat—or to ever have in the first place. From the moment she'd entered the trailer parked alongside the park ranger's office, she'd felt the tall, dark-haired officer's gaze fixed on her. She couldn't decide if he was rude or just overly intense; she hadn't spent a lot of time around law-enforcement types, so what did she know?

And what did she care? Except that the agent—Michael Dance—had made her care. He knew things about her she didn't. He knew what had happened in the hours and days she'd lost to unconsciousness and trauma. That he'd seen her ripped open and clinging to life by a thread felt so personal and intimate. She both resented him and wanted to know more.

As for Michael Dance, he seemed content to keep staring at her, and when she'd agreed to take the officers to the body she'd found, he'd slipped up beside her and insisted she ride with him.

"You could ride with me and Graham if you'd rather," Carmen, the only other woman in the room, offered, perhaps sensing Abby's unease.

"No, that's all right. I can ride with Lieutenant Dance." Alone in a vehicle, maybe she could ask him some of the questions that troubled her.

But now, as they cruised along the paved South Rim Road through the park, she felt tongue-tied and awkward.

He took a roll of Life Savers from the pocket of his uniform shirt and held it out to her. "Want one?"

"Okay." She took one of the butterscotch candies, then he did the same and returned the roll to his pocket.

"I'm addicted," he said. "I quit smoking last year and took up the candy as a substitute."

"Good for you for quitting," she said. "I knew a lot of soldiers who smoked, but I never took it up."

"Smart woman." He settled back in the driver's seat, gaze fixed on the curving ribbon of blacktop that skirted the park's main attraction—the deep, narrow Black Canyon.

Abby tried to relax, too, but curiosity needled her, overcoming her natural shyness. "How do you possibly remember me after all this time?" she blurted. "It's been years, and you must have only seen me for a few hours, at most." Had he been an orderly in the field hospital, a medic or a pilot, or simply a grunt tasked with transporting the wounded?

"I was a PJ. We saw hundreds of casualties during my tour—but you were the only woman. And you were my first save. It made an impression."

PJs—pararescuers—were bona fide superheroes. Members of the US Air Force's rescue squadron swooped into the thick of danger in Pave Hawk helicopters, often under heavy enemy fire, to snatch wounded soldiers from almost certain death. They performed critical lifesaving procedures in the air, long before their patients reached the doctors at field hospitals. Abby remembered none of this, but she'd seen a special on TV and watched with sick fascination, trying to imagine what it was like when she was the patient, being patched together by young men she'd likely never see again.

"I…I don't know what to say." She plucked at the seat belt harness, feeling trapped as much by her own emotions as by the confining cloth strap. "Thank you doesn't seem like enough."

"I was glad you made it. We lost too many soldiers over there, but losing a woman would have been worse. I know it shouldn't be that way, but it was—I won't lie."

She nodded. Though women weren't authorized for combat roles back then, the army needed female soldiers to interrogate native women and to fill a variety of noncombat roles, from resupply to repairing equipment that constantly broke down. Women soldiers stood guard and went on patrol, and sometimes got caught up in battles, in a war with no clearly defined front line, where every peasant could be friend or foe. But for all the roles they filled, women made up only about 10 percent of the ground forces in Afghanistan. As a female soldier, Abby hadn't wanted to stand out from her fellow grunts, but she couldn't help it.

"I still can't believe you remembered my name," she said.

He winced. "I made it a point to remember it. Later, I tried to look you up—just to see how you were doing. I'm not a stalker or anything. I just wanted to know."

"But you didn't find me?"

"I found out you'd gotten transferred stateside, but that was about it." He adjusted his grip on the steering wheel of the FJ Cruiser he drove. A second Cruiser followed a few car lengths behind, with Graham and Carmen; for all Abby knew half a dozen other vehicles full of more law-enforcement agents came after that. "But now I know. You look good. I'm glad."

She resisted the urge to touch the scar. "Thanks for not qualifying the compliment."

He frowned. "I don't get it."

"Thanks for not saying, 'You look good, considering what you've been through.'"

"People really tell you that?"

"Sometimes. I also get 'That scar is hardly noticeable,' which I know is a lie, since if it was so unnoticeable, why are they bothering to point it out?" Had she really just said that? To this guy she didn't even know? She didn't talk about this stuff with anybody. Not even the therapist the Army had sent her to. Waste of money, that.

"So you're studying botany?" Maybe sensing her uneasiness, he smoothly changed the subject.

"Environmental science. And to answer your next question, which I know from experience is, 'What do you do with a master's degree in environmental science?' I'll probably end up teaching ungrateful undergrads somewhere. But all that is just to support the research I want to do into developing medicines from plants."

"You mean, like herbal remedies and stuff?"

"I mean, like cancer drugs and medicine to cure Parkinson's or diabetes. Plants are a tremendous resource we've scarcely begun to explore."

"So there are plants in this park that can cure diseases?" He motioned to the scrubby landscape around them.

"This might look like desert to you, but there are

hundreds of plants within the park and surrounding public lands. It's the perfect place for my research."

"A big change from the war," he said.

"Everything is a big change from the war," she said. "Didn't you feel it, after you came home? That sense of not knowing what to do next? Of being a little out of place? Or was that just me?"

"It wasn't just you," he said. "Every day over there you had a mission—a purpose. Life over here isn't like that." He stared at the road ahead for a long moment, then added, "I thought about going back to school after I got out, but sitting in a classroom all day—that wasn't for me."

She shifted toward him, feeling more comfortable scrutinizing him for a change. He was good-looking—no doubt about that—with dark eyes and olive skin and a hawk nose and square chin. His broad shoulders filled out his short-sleeved tan shirt nicely, and slim-fit khakis showed off muscular thighs. "How did you end up working for border patrol?"

"They were at a job fair for veterans and it looked like interesting work. It was a lot of independent work, outdoors. I liked that."

She nodded. She understood that desire to be outdoors and alone, away from other people. After the noise, chaos and crowds of the war, the wilderness felt healing.

"It's great that you found work that's important," he said. "I mean, what you're doing could make a big difference in peoples' lives someday."

"Someday, maybe. But yeah, I do feel as though it's important work. Don't you think what you're doing is important?"

"Sometimes I do. Sometimes I'm not so sure." He checked his mirrors and crunched down on the candy. "You said this guy you found is Mexican?" he asked.

Back to the reason she was here. Guess they couldn't avoid that subject forever. "Well, Latino. He had dark hair and brown skin—like you."

"My mom is from Mexico. My dad's from Denver."

"Do you speak Spanish?"

"I do. Comes in handy on the job sometimes."

"Do you run into a lot of people from Mexico in the park?" she asked, thinking of Mariposa and Angelique.

"Some." He slowed as they reached the end of the paved road and bumped onto a rougher gravel surface. "How much farther from here?" he asked.

She checked her GPS. "About nine miles."

"You weren't kidding—remote."

"The best specimens are usually where they haven't been disturbed by people or grazing animals."

"Right. You haven't seen anything else suspicious while you were out and about this week, have you?"

She stiffened, again thinking of the Mexican woman and child. "What do you mean, suspicious?"

"A bunch of marijuana plants, for instance? Or a portable meth lab?"

"No. Should I have seen those things?"

"Probably not, if you want to stay safe."

"Is that why border patrol and the FBI and BLM and who knows who else are meeting in a trailer at park headquarters?" she asked. "To go after drugs in the park?"

The seat creaked as he shifted his weight. "We're an interagency task force formed to address rising crime in the park and surrounding lands—much of it drug related." He cut his eyes to her. "Just be careful out there. Good idea to carry that Sig."

"When I applied for my backcountry permit at the ranger station, they told me to watch out for snakes. No one said anything about drug dealers or murderers."

"Most tourists will never know they're there. And how many people who visit the park ever step off the main road or popular trails?"

"Not many," she said. "I almost never see anyone when I'm out in the backcountry." Which had made her encounter with Mariposa all the more remarkable. "If I do see anything suspicious, I'll stay far away," she said. "All I want to do is collect some plant specimens and get back to my research."

They both fell silent as the Cruiser bumped over the rutted, sometimes muddy road. Though it was already early June, most of the usually dry arroyos trickled with snowmelt, and grass that would later turn a papery brown looked green and lush. Abby spotted several small herds of deer grazing in the distance, and a cluster of pronghorn antelope that exploded into life as the vehicles trundled past, bouncing away in stiff-legged leaps.

Finally her GPS indicated they were near the area where she'd found the body. "Pull over anywhere," she said. "We'll have to walk in from here."

Michael stopped the Cruiser alongside the road and Graham slid his vehicle in behind them. The officers opened up the backs of the Cruisers and pulled out packs, canteens and, in Graham's case, a semiautomatic rifle. They were going in loaded for bear, she supposed in case they ran into any of the bad guys.

Graham indicated she should lead the way. GPS in

hand, she set out walking. The officers fell in behind in classic patrol formation. Abby's heart raced. She slipped her hand into the front pocket of her jeans and wrapped it around the rabbit charm. *Nothing to worry about*, she reminded herself. *You're in Colorado. In a national park. No snipers here.*

But of course, the dead man she'd found earlier reminded her that the serene landscape was not as safe as it seemed.

They walked for an hour before they came to the patch of desert parsley she'd harvested earlier. She noted the freshly turned earth where she'd dug up her specimen. "There's the boulder I hid behind." She pointed to the large rock, then walked over to it, trying to remember everything she'd done in those moments before she discovered the body. "I started walking this way."

She led the way, the other three moving silently behind her. A few minutes later she spotted the pink bandanna she'd left tied to the branch of a piñon. "There." She pointed. "The body is by that tree."

She stopped and let the three officers move past.

She watched from a distance as they surveyed the body. Carmen took a number of photographs, then they fanned out, searching the ground—for clues, she supposed. She stood in the shade of the piñon, wishing she were anywhere else. She'd thought she'd put killing and bodies behind her when she left Afghanistan. The wilderness was supposed to be a place of peace, not violence.

Michael returned to her side. "You doing okay?" he asked.

She nodded. "I'll be fine."

She felt his gaze on her, but he didn't press, for which

she was grateful. "Which direction did the men you saw come from?" he asked after a moment.

"From over there, near that wash." She nodded in the direction of the shallow depression in the terrain.

Graham joined them. "We'll need to seal off this area and send a team out to collect evidence."

"We need to figure out where he came from," Michael said. "There might be a camp somewhere nearby."

"Where are you camped, Ms. Stewart?" Graham asked.

"I'm in the South Rim Campground."

"Let us know if you decide to move into town or return to your home, in case we have questions," Graham said.

"I'd planned to stay here for another week to ten days," she said. "I've only just begun collecting the specimens I need."

"This part of the park will be off-limits to the public for most of that time, I'm afraid," Graham said. "Until we determine it's safe."

He was going to close the backcountry? "That really isn't acceptable," she said. "I'm not some naive tourist, stumbling around, but I really need to collect these specimens to complete my research."

"You'll have to find them somewhere else. Until I decide it's safe, this section of the park is closed."

The three officers studied her, expressions impassive, implacable. She turned away, and her gaze fell on the body on the ground. All she could see was the feet, but they lay there with the stillness of a mannequin. Lifeless, a cruel joke played out in the desert.

She hated having her plans thwarted, but she knew Graham and the others were right. Until they knew who had killed this man and why, they had to err on the side of caution. "Fine. There are other places in the backcountry where I can look for specimens."

"Let us know…"

But Graham never finished the sentence. Bark exploded from the trunk of a tree beside her. "Get down!" Michael yelled, and shoved her to the ground as bullets whistled over their heads.

Chapter Four

In the silence that followed the burst of gunfire, the drum of Michael's pulse in his ears was so loud he was sure everyone could hear it. He slowed his breathing and strained his ears, alert for any clue about the shooter. Beneath him, Abby shifted, and he became aware of her ragged breathing. She shoved and he realized he was crushing her. Better crushed than shot, he thought, but he eased up a fraction of an inch, putting more of his weight on his hands, braced on the ground beneath his shoulders, and his knees, straddled on either side of her.

They lay in a depression in the ground, a shallow wash pocked with rocks and low scrub and a few stunted piñons. Turning his head, Michael spotted Graham and Carmen about five feet away. His eyes met Graham's. The supervisor looked angry enough to chew nails.

"Who's shooting at us?" Abby whispered, her voice so low he wondered at first if he'd imagined the question.

"Sniper," Graham answered. "I make his hide site about three hundred yards to the south, on that slight rise."

Michael turned his head, but he couldn't see anything except grass and dirt and the trunk of a piñon. They were too exposed here for him to even lift his head.

"He must be wearing a ghillie suit," Carmen said. "I can't see a thing." Michael turned back to look at her and realized she was half sitting behind a boulder. She'd pulled binoculars from her pack and was scanning the area.

"What's someone out here doing with a ghillie suit?" Abby asked.

Michael had been wondering the same thing. In a training course he'd taken, he'd seen men in the cumbersome camouflage suits covered with twigs and leaves so that when the wearer froze, he blended in completely with the surrounding landscape. It wasn't something you could pick up at your local outdoor supplier.

"They could have stolen one from the military, or made their own," Graham said. "These drug operations spare no expense to protect their business. That sniper rifle he's got is probably military issue, or close to it."

Graham shifted, reaching for his radio; the movement was enough to draw another blast of gunfire, bullets spitting into the dirt in front of them. Abby flinched, jolting against Michael. "Are you okay?" he whispered.

"Just a rock on my cheek. It's nothing."

More gunfire exploded, this time to their right. From her vantage point behind the boulder, Carmen had returned fire. "He's too far away," she said, lowering the weapon.

"Ranger Two, this is Ranger One, do you copy?" Graham had used the distraction to retrieve the radio from his utility belt and key the mike.

"Ranger Two. I copy." Simon's voice crackled through the static.

"We're pinned down by a sniper in the backcountry." He recited the GPS coordinates Abby had given them for her plant find. "Looks like one shooter. His hide site is approximately three hundred yards south of our position. He's on a small rise, maybe wearing a ghillie suit."

"We're on it. We'll try to come in behind him."

"Roger that. Over." Graham laid the radio on the ground beside his head. "Now we wait," he said.

Michael tried to ignore the cramping in his arms. If he let up, he'd crush Abby again, but any movement was liable to draw the sniper's fire. "Sorry," he said to her. "I know this isn't the most comfortable position."

She didn't answer. Instead, she started to tremble, tremors running through her body into his. She made a muffled sound, almost like…sobbing.

The sound tore at him. The sight of the dead man hadn't moved him, and while the sniper's fire got his adrenaline pumping, it didn't shake him the way Abby's sorrow did. "Hey." He slid one hand to her shoulder and turned his head so that his mouth was next to her ear. He spoke softly, not wanting the others to hear. "It's okay," he said. "Our team is good. They'll nail this guy."

She tensed, her fingers digging into the dirt beneath them. Her breathing was ragged, and he could sense panic rising off her in waves. Was she having some kind of flashback? How could he help her—comfort her?

He'd been shot at plenty of times as a PJ, but they always had the Pave Hawks to swoop them out of danger. He'd always been too focused on the mission, on saving lives, to worry much about his own. It must have been worse for troops on the ground, like her.

He tried to lift more of his weight off her. "Hey," he said again. "Abby, talk to me. You're going to be okay."

She sucked in a ragged breath, her body rising and falling beneath him. "I hate this," she said after a minute.

"I hate it, too." The words sounded lame, even to him, but he'd say anything to keep her talking. "But you'll be okay. The cavalry is on its way."

The muscles of her cheek against his shifted; he hoped she was smiling at his lame joke. "This is probably the last thing you expected when you came out here to dig plants," he said.

"Yeah." The shaking wasn't as violent now—only a tremor shuddering through her every now and then. Her hands had relaxed, no longer gripping the dirt. He resisted the urge to smooth his hand along her back; she might take it the wrong way. As it was, he was becoming all too aware of the feel of her body beneath his, the side of her breast nestled beside his arm, the soft curve of her backside against his groin.

"This is just a little too familiar," she said.

He realized she wasn't talking about the feel of their bodies pressed together. "You've been pinned down by a sniper before?"

"Oh, yeah. That was the thing about being over there—the unpredictability of it all—not knowing when an IED would explode or a sniper would fire, not knowing who you could trust."

You can trust me, he wanted to say. But he didn't. Trusting him didn't change the fact that there was somebody they couldn't see determined to kill them if they so much as lifted their heads. He hadn't done a very good job so far of protecting her. The best he could hope for was to provide a distraction. "Have you always been interested in plants?" he asked. "Did you always plan to study biology?"

"I was going to be a television news anchor," she said. "Or a model. This scar on my face put an end to that."

Only a deaf man would miss the bitterness in her words. She was certainly pretty enough to be a model—but she probably didn't want to hear that, either. He tried once more to get the conversation back on track. "What you're doing now—finding plants that could cure cancer. That sounds a lot more rewarding."

"Yeah." She fell silent again. Okay, so she didn't want to talk. At least she'd stopped shaking.

"Mostly, I like the solitude," she said after a moment. "It's so peaceful out here. Usually."

"Yeah. Usually it is. You just got lucky."

She actually chuckled then—the sound made him feel about ten feet tall, as if he'd done something a lot more heroic than make lame jokes.

"Why do you think he's shooting at us?" she asked. "Is it because we found the dead man?"

"I doubt it's that. My guess is the dead guy's an illegal. He won't have any ID on him, or anything to tie him to anyone or anything. Most likely the sniper is protecting something. A meth lab or something like that."

"But doesn't firing at us give away the fact that there's something out here worth protecting?"

"Yeah, but it keeps us from getting too close and buys them time to move the operation. When we finally make it out to investigate, whatever is going on will be long gone."

"What happens after that?"

"We have a starting place for our search. From there we try to track them to their new location."

"Like in the war," she said.

"Yeah. A lot like in the war."

"Just my dumb luck that I come out here to get away from all that and end up in the middle of it. Do you ever feel that way?" she asked.

"Yeah," he said. "I thought my job would mostly be inspecting shipments and checking passports— looking for drugs and illegals, for sure. I knew I'd carry a weapon, but I didn't expect to ever have to use it. But then I think, maybe I'm exactly where I'm supposed to be. Maybe my military training can help me put an end to some of the violence, at least."

"Do you really believe that?" she asked. "That things happen for a reason?"

"Yeah. I mean, don't you think it's more than coincidence that we met up again after all this time?" Five years in which he'd never really forgotten about her. "I mean, what are the odds?"

"That's why it's called a coincidence," she said. "It's random. Just like me ending up out here in the middle of your little drug war. It's the way life works, but it doesn't mean anything."

MICHAEL DIDN'T SAY anything after Abby shot down his theory that the two of them were meant to meet up again. Well, sorry, but she didn't believe in fate. She wasn't meant to be flat on her stomach, squashed by some big guy in fatigues while another guy took pot-shots at her, any more than she was meant to disappoint her family by becoming a recluse who wandered the desert in search of rare plants. Life was life. Things happened and you rolled with the punches. She liked looking for plants in the desert, and she hoped the work she did now would help somebody else someday. But that didn't mean she'd been guided by fate. She made her own choices and accepted the consequences.

She closed her eyes, thinking she might as well catch a nap while she waited for whatever Michael's partners were doing out there. But closing her eyes was a mistake. As soon as her eyelids descended, she was back in Kandahar, pinned down by a sniper, her face in the dirt just like it was now. Only back then, there had been no cavalry to come to the rescue—the rest of her unit had been pinned down by enemy fire or already wiped out. For six hours she'd lain there with her face in the dirt while the guy next to her silently bled out and the guy on her other side freaked out, sobbing like a baby until every nerve in her was raw. In the end, the shooter must have decided they were all dead and moved on. Her own company thought the same thing—she woke up with two men slinging her onto a stretcher and someone shouting, "Hey, we've got a live one here!"

She opened her eyes again. Time to think about something else. Mariposa. Where were she and Angelique right now? Was she safe? Was she somehow mixed up in whatever illegal operation the sniper was protecting? What was she—somebody's wife or girlfriend, along for the ride, in over her head now? Was she as surprised by the violence that intruded on such peaceful surroundings as Abby was?

"When you were out here before, collecting your plants, did you see anybody else?" Michael asked. "Besides the men who were after our dead guy?"

What was he, a mind reader or something? "No, I didn't see anybody," she lied.

"No other hikers or campers?"

"I saw two hikers three days ago. They were tourists from Australia. And I pass people on the roads and see campers in the campground."

"That's it?"

"Why? Don't you believe me?"

"In interrogation training, they tell you that if you ask the same question in several different ways, you sometimes get different answers."

"So now you're interrogating me?" What she wouldn't give to be able to look him in the eye when she spoke. Instead, she was forced to address the ground while he lay on top of her. She appreciated that he was doing his best to hold himself off her, but still, the guy was big and solid. An easy one hundred and eighty pounds.

"It's a harsh word for questioning," he said. "A lot of law enforcement is just asking the right questions, of victims, or witnesses, or suspects."

"Well, you're not going to get different answers from me." She saw no reason to betray Mariposa to him. "Do you think you could just slide off me?" she asked.

"I don't think we'd better risk it. Movement seems to set off our shooter."

"Why did you throw yourself on top of me in the first place?"

"I'm trained to protect civilians. And I don't care how politically incorrect it is, my instincts are to keep women and children out of harm's way."

"How chivalrous of you." She hesitated, then added, "But thanks, all the same." The one thing she'd missed about the military was that sense that her buddies had her back.

"You're welcome. Sorry we couldn't have gotten re-acquainted under better circumstances."

"Now that he's not actually shooting at us and we're just waiting, it's pretty boring," she said. "Like most of the time in the war."

"Are all our conversations going to come back to that?" he asked.

"Does it bother you, talking about the war?"

"Not really. I thought it bothered you."

"Sometimes it does," she admitted. When other people asked about her experiences in Afghanistan, she deflected the questions or changed the subject. "It's easier with you. You were over there. You understand."

"I guess I do relate to what you went through. A little bit anyway."

The radio's crackle made them both flinch. Abby turned her head toward the sound. Graham keyed the mike. "What have you got?" he asked.

"All clear here." One of the team members—maybe the sour-faced guy, Simon—said.

"No sign of the shooter?" Graham asked.

"Somebody was here, all right. There's broken brush and we found some shell casings. Looks like a .300 Win Mag. The dirt's a little scuffed up, but the ground's too hard to leave much of an impression."

"Get Randall and Lotte on it."

"They're here. The dog picked up a scent, but it died at the road. We found some tire tracks that look like a truck. We figure someone was waiting to pick up our guy. We never saw signs of a vehicle, so he probably left not long after he fired the last shots at y'all."

Graham swore under his breath and shoved up onto his knees. No gunshots split the air. Abby let out the breath she hadn't even realized she'd been holding.

Michael rolled off her and popped to his feet, then reached out a hand to help her up. She let him pull her up, her limbs stiff and sore from so long being prone. Clearly, she wasn't in as good a shape as she'd thought. "You're bleeding," he said, and gently touched the side of her face.

She flinched as his fingers brushed against the scar, but then she felt the stickiness of already drying blood. "A rock ricocheted off the ground," she said. "It's nothing."

"Here." He handed her a black bandanna, then offered a bottle of water. "You should clean it up."

Head down, she accepted the water and dampened the bandanna. The square of cloth was clean and crisp, like something a businessman would carry tucked into his pocket. She turned her back to the others as she cleaned off the blood and dirt from the side of her face.

"Let me have a look." Michael moved around in front of her. "You may need stitches."

"It's nothing." She tried once more to turn away, but he put his hand on her shoulder and took her chin in his other hand. "It's okay," he said softly. "I promise I don't faint at the sight of blood."

The teasing quality of the words almost made her smile. If anyone had seen her at her worst, it had been this guy. She had no idea what she'd looked like when the PJs had hauled her onto that helicopter, but the doctors had told her the shrapnel from the IED had torn through the side of her face, narrowly missing her eye.

As much as she hated the scar, it was nothing compared to how she might have ended up.

She let him lift her chin and study the side of her face.

"It's just a little cut, pretty shallow. When we get back to the truck I'll get a bandage for it."

"Thanks." She turned away and combed her hair down to cover the side of her face again.

"Get Marco to help you with recon," Graham said. "I'll notify the park rangers that the backcountry is closed indefinitely. No more permits, and they'll need to round up anyone out with a permit now. Over."

"You mean just the backcountry within the park, right?" Abby asked.

"I mean all the park, the recreation area and Gunnison Gorge. If these people have a sniper looking after their interests, they have some real money and muscle behind it. Until we know the scope of their operation, we can't risk the safety of the public."

"You can't expect to keep people out of an area that large," she said.

"We can't prevent all unauthorized access, but we can stop issuing permits and close all the roads leading into the area. I'm sorry, but that means you won't be able to continue your research in the area."

His tone of command left little room for argument. He looked past her to Michael. "Take her back to headquarters, then meet up with Simon and the others. Ms. Stewart, we may have more questions for you later."

She doubted she'd have any useful answers, but she only nodded and turned to follow Michael back to the Cruiser. By the time they reached the vehicle, she was fuming.

"Sorry about your research," Michael said as he started the truck. "Maybe you can come back and finish up next summer. Hopefully, things will have calmed down by then."

"I don't have next summer," she said. "My grant is for this summer. Next summer I'll have to find a job and start paying off my student loans."

"Is there someplace else you can research—another park, or another part of the state?"

"My grant is to explore this area. Shifting my focus requires a new grant application. Your commander is overreacting. He doesn't have to close off all one hundred and thirty thousand acres of public land. That's ridiculous."

"Can you blame him? He's already under the gun from politicians who think this task force is a waste of money—can you imagine the fallout if some tourist gets taken out by a sniper? We've already got one murder on our hands. Your plants will still be there when this investigation is over."

"Don't patronize me."

"I'm not patronizing. I'm just trying to get you to calm down."

His words only made her more furious. She did not need to calm down. She'd just been shot at and forced to lie on her stomach on the ground for over an hour, and suffered the humiliation of almost flaking out in front of a bunch of strangers—if she didn't give vent to the tornado of emotions inside of her she might explode. "Shut up," she said. "Whatever you have to say, I don't want to hear it."

He glared at her for a long moment, then turned his attention to the road. The truck rocketed forward, bouncing over the rough two-track so that she had to grip the handle mounted at the top of the door to steady herself. Dust boiled up behind them, and rocks pinged against the undercarriage like BBs. She clenched her jaw to keep from shouting at him to slow down and not be so reckless. But that was what he wanted from her—another reaction. She wouldn't give him the satisfaction.

She'd already let him affect her emotions too much, his combination of brashness and consideration, strength and tenderness, touching vulnerable places inside her she hadn't let anyone see. She never talked about the war with anyone, and yet she'd confided in him. She didn't willingly let others see her scars, but she'd turned her face up to him with only a moment's hesitation. She didn't like how open and undefended he made her feel, with all his talk of fate and meaning behind what had to be only coincidence.

After a few miles, he slowed down enough that she could relax back in the seat. She hugged her arms across her chest and stared out at the landscape. Most people probably thought the land was ugly, with its scraggly vegetation and covering of rock and thin dirt. The real treasure lay beneath eye level, in the startlingly deep, narrow canyon that cut a jagged swath through the high desert, its walls painted in shades of red and orange and gray. People long ago had dubbed it the Black Canyon, since sunlight seldom reached its depths. The silvery ribbon of the Gunnison River rushed through the bottom of the canyon, nurturing lush growth along its rocky banks, creating a world of color and moisture far below the parched landscape above.

But that stark desert held as much interest for Abby as the canyon below. She'd enjoyed discovering the secrets of the twisted piñons and miniature wildflowers, learning about the deer, rabbits, foxes and other wildlife that thrived there. She thought of herself like them— someone who had learned to survive amid bareness, to find the beauty in hardship.

They pulled up in front of headquarters. Her car was the only one in the lot now. She unsnapped her seat belt and her hand was on the door when Michael spoke. "Look. It isn't safe for you to go into the back-country by yourself, but what if I went with you? You can look for your plants while I patrol. I can square it with Graham."

She could only imagine the pushback he'd get from his supervisor when he made that suggestion. Captain Graham Ellison struck her as a man who wasn't into bending the rules. "Why would you do that?"

He shrugged. "I kind of feel responsible for you."

Wrong answer. She didn't want anyone—she especially didn't want this man—to be responsible for her. She was responsible for herself. She climbed out of the truck and turned to face him. "I get that you saved my life," she said. "And I'm grateful for that. But that doesn't give you any kind of special claim on me."

He held up both hands. "I'm not making any claim on you. I'm just trying to help."

"I don't need your help. Thanks anyway." She turned and stalked away, though she could feel his gaze burning into her all the way to her car.

Chapter Five

"We got nothing." Simon slapped a thin file folder onto the conference room table and sank into a chair, a look of disgust on his face.

Graham, seated at the head of the table, frowned and reached for the folder. "What do you mean, you've got nothing?" he said. "We've got a dead body. We've got shell casings from a gun—tire tracks. All of that must lead to something." He leveled his stern gaze on the others around the table. Michael unwrapped another Life Saver and popped it into his mouth. Already, this meeting was off to a bad start. Twenty-four hours in and they had no more to go on than they had when Abby had walked into their office yesterday afternoon.

"It leads nowhere," Simon said. "The man had no ID. His fingerprints aren't in any database. We sent in DNA, but I doubt it will come up with anything—he's obviously an illegal. We're not even sure where he's from. Could be Mexico, Central America, South America…" He shook his head.

"Where he's from may not be important," Graham said, tapping the file, which he hadn't bothered to open. "I want to know why he was shot in the middle of nowhere like that, and who shot him."

"Somebody wanted to shut him up."

All heads turned toward Marco, who had spoken. "Shut him up why?" Graham asked.

"I think he was trying to escape and they silenced him," Marco said.

"Why not bring him back?" Randall asked. "If our theory is these illegals are brought here to work in some drug operation, why lose a good worker?"

"A man who wants to get away badly enough to take off across the wilderness on foot isn't a good worker," Marco said.

"With this level of security, I'd say we're definitely looking at a drug operation," Simon said. "So why can't we find it?"

"If it's meth, it could be in a little trailer camouflaged on the back of beyond," Michael said. "Even if it's a grow op, they can hide acres of the stuff in remote canyons."

"Our aerial patrols haven't spotted anything suspicious." Graham's chair creaked as he leaned back in it. "Did Lotte pick up any scent?"

The Belgian Malinois raised her head, alert. Randall dropped his hand to idly stroke her head. "She worked for a couple of hours yesterday, but none of the trails she picked up led to anything."

"What about Abby Stewart?"

Michael realized Graham had addressed him. "What about her?" he asked.

"She's the one who found the body, and she was with us when the sniper fired," Graham said. "What's her link to all this?"

"She was in the wrong place at the wrong time," Michael said. "No link."

"What do we know about her?" Simon asked. "Is she really who she says she is?"

"She's who I say she is." Michael tried to suppress his annoyance and failed. "I knew her in Afghanistan. She was wounded over there, came home to recuperate and now she's a student at University of Colorado, earning her master's in biology."

"Her story checks out," Carmen said. "She came to the park five days ago and requested a backcountry permit. The park rangers told me she goes out every morning and comes back in the evening with her notebooks, pack and specimens she's collected."

"She could be meeting with anyone in that time," Simon said.

"You checked her out?" Michael's stomach churned, as if he'd been the subject of their snooping.

"We check everyone out," Graham said. "How was she when she left you yesterday?"

She'd been furious with him. If looks could kill, he'd be seriously wounded right now. "She was upset about not being able to continue her research," he said. "She has a grant that runs out at the end of the summer."

"What's she researching anyway?" Randall asked.

"Plants that grow in this area that have medicinal purposes," Michael said. "She says stuff that grows out there could be used to treat or cure cancer and other diseases."

"Sounds like a good excuse to spend time in the backcountry," Simon said. "Maybe the plant she's really interested in is marijuana."

"There are a lot of plants that have medicinal uses," Carmen said. "My people have known that for centuries. You palefaces are just now figuring it out."

Simon ignored the dig and leaned across the table toward Michael. "Even if she's not involved with our killers, that sniper saw her with us yesterday. He'll report that to his handlers."

"If they think she witnessed something out there, they'll want to shut her up, too," Marco said.

Michael felt as if he'd swallowed ice. "She could be in danger."

"It's a possibility," Graham said. "We'll need to keep an eye on her."

"I offered to take her out on patrol with me," Michael said. "That way, she could collect her plants and I could make sure she didn't wander into anything dangerous."

"Not a bad idea," Graham said. "What did she think?"

"She was still pretty shaken up by the sniper thing." No sense admitting he'd blown it by coming on too strong. "She had some bad experiences in the war."

"You said she almost died?" Carmen asked.

"She did die." Michael didn't have to close his eyes to see her lying on that stretcher, pale as the sheets. "She coded in the helicopter on the way to the hospital. We brought her back, but she was pretty messed up."

"She was hit in the face?" Carmen stroked the side of her own face.

"She was hit all over, but the head wound was the worst."

"And you saved her life," Carmen said.

He looked away. "I did my job."

"Then you have a connection with her, whether she acknowledges that or not," Graham said. "Go talk to her. Tell her we want to offer her protection, in exchange for her help."

"What kind of help?" The idea surprised him.

"I have a sense she knows something she's not telling us," Graham said. He opened the file. "Now let's see if there's anything else in here we can go after."

"I'm doing fine, Dad. The research is going well." Abby held the phone tightly to her ear and paced the length of the travel trailer she'd rented for the summer. Four steps toward the bedroom at one end, turn and four steps back to the dinette at the other end, passing the galley kitchen in between. The research had been going well, until Michael Dance and his friends had thrown a wrench in her plans.

"Have you thought any more about coming home when you've wrapped things up there?" Her dad's voice, the velvety, well-modulated bass that was familiar to sports fans and channel-four viewers all over Milwaukee, seemed to fill up the trailer. "I've been talking to some people I know at the station. We've got a vacancy for a weekend anchor job. They'd love to give you a tryout."

Abby squeezed her eyes shut and suppressed a groan. "That wouldn't be a good idea, Dad." Any tryout they gave her would be because her dad—Brian Stewart, the voice of Milwaukee sports—had called in favors. Or worse, because they were playing the wounded-vet card. She wanted no part of it.

"Nonsense! You were always a natural in front of the camera. And if you're worried about your scar—it really isn't that bad. Stage makeup can cover a lot, you know, and you could have more plastic surgery."

How many times had he said the same thing? Did he

not hear her when she talked? "No more surgery," she said. "And no makeup. This is who I am."

"At least think about it. You know it would mean a lot to me."

And of course, this is all about you. She didn't say the words out loud. She wasn't that cruel. Practically since she could talk, her father had built the dream of her following in his footsteps. All the beauty pageants, the voice lessons and drama camps, had been part of his plan to turn her into an even bigger celebrity than he was.

"Are you sure you're okay, honey?" he asked. "You sound tired."

Maybe because she'd hardly slept last night, kept awake by memories of the day's events, mingled with flashbacks to the war. In the dark hours of the early morning, it had been hard to differentiate between the two. But she mentioned none of this to her father. He'd freak out and it would only prove what he had been saying for months now—that she was crazy to throw her life away on plants. Not when she had so much talent.

But did she really have talent? She had spent so many years getting by on her good looks. When you were blessed with beauty, people never looked any deeper or expected anything more. Their impression of you stayed on the surface. At least now when she made a discovery, she knew it was because she'd used her brain. "I'll be fine, Dad. It was good talking to you. I'd better go now. I have work to do."

"Goodbye, sweetheart. I love you. Your mom sends her love, too."

"I love you, too, Dad. Talk to you soon." She clicked off the phone and slid it into her pocket, then stared out the window at the distant mountains, the peaks still capped with snow. Maybe when she won the Nobel Prize for her work with medicinal plants, her father would give up his dream of making her a star, though she doubted it.

Knocking on the door of the little trailer startled her. She glanced at the gun, in its holster on the counter by the door, within easy reach if she needed it, then peeled back a corner of the blinds in the window beside the door.

Michael Dance stood on the ground below the steps, eyes shaded by dark sunglasses. He rocked back on his heels and glanced around the campsite, then leaned forward to knock again. She pulled open the door. "Good afternoon," she said.

"Good afternoon to you, too." His smile dazzled. It hit her like a spotlight, or maybe more like a laser beam, warmth blossoming in her chest.

"Come on in." She stepped back to let him pass her.

He stood in the middle of the trailer's one room and looked around—at the compact dinette with the padded bench seats all around that she used as a desk, at the half-size refrigerator and compact stove, microwave and sink, and back to the closed door of the bathroom and the queen-size bed. He nodded in approval. "This is nice. Cozy."

"It serves its purpose." She slid past him, the narrow space forcing them to brush together, the brief contact sending another wash of heat through her. She sat at the dinette, shoved her laptop to one side and motioned to the seat across from her. "Make yourself at home."

He eased his big frame onto the bench. "I didn't

mean to interrupt your work," he said, nodding to the laptop.

"I was just compiling the notes I've made so far. And cataloging my specimens, since I don't know when I'll be able to collect more."

"Listen, about yesterday—" he began.

"I'm sorry I went off on you like that," she said. "I was still upset about the sniper and finding that dead man and…and everything. I shouldn't have taken it out on you."

She was touched by how relieved he looked. "I understand," he said. "It was a lot to take in. Most people would be overwhelmed."

"I should have handled it better." After all, she'd had plenty of practice dealing with death and violence in her short time in the military.

"The offer to come with me on patrol is still open," he said.

Relief washed over her. She'd been prepared to beg if she had to, in order to continue her research. "Then, I accept."

"Great." He drummed his fingers on the table and looked around the trailer once more, avoiding her gaze.

"Is there something else?" she asked.

His eyes shifted back to her. "The G-Man— Graham—thinks there's something you're not telling us. About yesterday, when that man was shot."

So much for her acting ability. Or maybe it was just that she was having second thoughts about keeping her secret. What if Mariposa was somehow tied up with whatever was going on out there in the parkland? By not telling about her, was Abby endangering other peoples' lives?

"Before I tell you anything else, answer a few questions for me first," she said.

He sat back, hands flat on the table between them. "All right."

She couldn't look into that intense gaze anymore, so she studied his hands. He had long fingers and neatly trimmed nails, and he wore a silver-and-onyx ring on his right hand. They were masculine, capable hands—she remembered the feel of them at her back yesterday. Reassuring. Protective. "You work for Customs and Immigration, right?"

"US Customs and Border Protection."

"So when you encounter someone who's in this country illegally, your job is to deport them?"

"That's more Simon's territory. He's with ICE—Immigration and Customs Enforcement. They're part of Homeland Security, too. My job is more about protecting our borders, though we work with ICE sometimes. Why?"

She shifted in her seat. How to admit to this man that she'd been lying to him? "I did see someone else yesterday—before the man was shot. There was a woman. She was out collecting plants, too, but for food, not for scientific specimens. She spoke only Spanish and she had a baby with her. She told me her name was Mariposa. She was so young—and gorgeous. I wouldn't have stood a chance if I'd competed in a pageant with her. Here, I have a picture." She pulled her phone from her pocket and found the photo she'd snapped of Mariposa. She handed the phone to him.

"She looks young," he said. "A teenager."

"Maybe," Abby said.

He returned the phone to her. "She trusted you enough to let you take her picture."

"I didn't ask, I just snapped it in between shots of the plants I was gathering. She seemed surprised, but she didn't object."

"We'll run the photo by authorities, but I doubt we'll find anything," he said. "Still, you never know. Did she say where she lived? What she was doing out there?"

"No. Like I said, she didn't speak English and I don't know much Spanish. I gave her a couple of protein bars and she seemed grateful. She heard the people who shot that man shouting and she took off. I mean, she panicked and was running for her life."

"So she knew who they were?"

"That's what I think. Or at least what they were up to." She touched the back of his hand. "Do you think she's mixed up in all this somehow? Maybe she's being held prisoner by these people or something?"

"She's probably one of the workers. These drug operations bring illegals in to work their grow operations or make meth. They're as good as prisoners, isolated out here, kept under guard."

"Is that what happened to that man—he tried to escape?"

"We don't know for sure, but that's a likely scenario."

"No wonder she panicked and ran."

"Did she say anything else?"

"She said the baby was a girl named Angelique. And she showed me where to find some of the plants I was looking for. She seemed very familiar with the plants in the area. I got the impression she was hungry." She blinked back tears, thinking of the beautiful woman and the baby, alone and in danger.

"Maybe we can find her and help her. Even if we send her back to her home, that would be better than the way she's living now."

"I guess so." Better to return to home and family than to live with the threat of danger.

"You competed in beauty pageants?" Michael asked.

Of course he'd picked up on that. Why had she even mentioned it? "Don't sound so shocked. I was Miss Milwaukee my freshman year in college."

"How did a beauty queen end up in Afghanistan?"

"It's a long story."

"I've got time."

She sighed. She could try to blow him off, but he struck her as someone who wouldn't give up questioning her. It was probably a trait that made him good at his job. "I thought it would be a good way to get money for grad school," she said. "My parents thought I was wasting my time with more schooling, so they wouldn't pay. And I didn't expect them to. I was willing to do it on my own."

"So the beauty queen wanted to be a biologist all along," he said.

"I didn't know what I wanted to do," she said. "My undergrad degree is in communications. But I needed to get away from home. My father is a local celebrity. He does sports for the number one news station in the city, plus he does a lot of voice-over work—ads and public service announcements and things. Everybody knows him. He wanted me to follow in his footsteps, but I wanted the chance to prove myself doing something that was just mine. I never thought it would turn out the way it did."

"No one does," he said. "I mean, you couldn't, right?

No one would enlist if the first thing that came to mind was dying or being injured."

"My parents were horrified—first with my enlistment, then when I went overseas. When I was injured they freaked out. My mother burst into tears the first time she saw the scar. She still can hardly bear to look at me." She swallowed past the tightness in her throat. "My dad is always trying to fix me. He wants me to have more surgery, to try special makeup. He can't let go of the hope that I'll go into television after all. They think I'm wasting my time trying to be a scientist."

"Do you think it's a waste of time?"

"No. I'm happier doing this—something that's all mine—than I would have been competing with my dad. And I would have been competing, at least subconsciously. This is a chance to prove myself on my own terms. I guess it's what I was looking for in the military all along."

"Funny sometimes, how life has a way of working out."

"If you're talking about fate, I still don't believe in that. Things just happen for no reason."

"Hey, I didn't say anything." He grinned. "Is tomorrow soon enough for us to go out?"

"Go out?" She blushed, and hated that she did so.

"On patrol. You said you wanted to come with me, right?"

On patrol—of course. What was she, some sixteen-year-old expecting the class jock to ask her out on a date? "Oh, yeah. Sure. When can we go?"

"I'll pick you up about eight." He stood, and she rose, also, and followed him to the door. "Thanks for telling me about Mariposa," he said. "We'll try to find her and help her."

"I should have trusted you earlier, but…"

"Yeah, I know. It's hard to trust sometimes."

She followed him out the door, reluctant to say good-bye. Now that she'd confided in him, she felt closer somehow. As if she finally had a friend who really understood her. "What's that on your car?" he asked.

She followed his gaze to the box sitting on the hood of the Toyota Camry. "I don't know. I've never seen it before."

They walked to the car and she started to reach for the box, but he put out his arm to stop her. "Don't touch it yet. Let's take a closer look."

Following his example, she leaned over and read the writing on the outside of the small brown cardboard box. *Abby Stewart* was written in marker in block letters. "I don't see anything that says who it's from," she said.

"So you're not expecting a package from anyone?"

"No." She wrapped her arms across her stomach, fighting back a wave of nausea at the idea that a stranger had walked into her camp and left this.

Michael pulled out his radio. "Let's get Randall and Lotte over to take a look."

"The dog? Do you really think that's necessary?" She eyed the box. It looked both innocent and sinister.

"Better to be safe."

He made the call and Randall said he'd be right over. They retreated to the shade of the trailer's awning to wait. Abby fidgeted, but Michael leaned against the trailer, relaxed. "It's probably nothing," she said. "Maybe we should just open it."

"Let's wait," he said, and she didn't argue.

Randall pulled in beside Michael's Cruiser a few minutes later. He got out of the truck, then released Lotte. She trotted forward, eyes bright, tail waving. Randall showed her the box. "Lotte, *such*," he commanded.

The dog braced her front paws on the bumper of the car and stretched toward the box, ears flattened, tail low. She retreated quickly, whining, and circled the vehicle, clearly agitated. She paced, panting and whining, looking from the box to Randall and back again. "She doesn't look too happy about whatever is in there," Michael said.

"She's not alerting for bombs or explosives," Randall said. "But she doesn't like whatever she's smelling. Lotte, *komm*."

The dog came and lay at Randall's side. Michael took out a knife. "Let's see what we've got."

He picked up the box and balanced it in his hands. "It's heavy," he said. "Maybe three or four pounds." He opened out a blade on the knife and slit the tape along the sides of the box, then set it on the ground. "Better play it safe." He picked up a stick from beside the campsite's picnic table. "Stand back."

Abby retreated a few steps, chewing her lip nervously. They were probably going through all this drama for nothing, but the dog's behavior worried her. Whatever was in that box, it had upset Lotte, who still stared at it, her brow wrinkled.

Michael slid the tip of the stick under the edge of the box lid, and with a jerk, flipped it off. The box tilted to its side, the contents pouring out in a rippling, fluid motion. Lotte barked, and Abby screamed as she stared at the huge rattler, coiled and ready to strike.

Chapter Six

Michael pulled out his service weapon and squeezed off two shots. The rattler writhed and thrashed, then lay still. Lotte barked again and whined. Despite the heat, Abby felt chilled through. She stared at the dead snake, shaken more by the idea that someone had intended it for her than by the snake itself.

A gust of wind rattled the branches of the piñons that surrounded the campsite, and tugged at the awning of the trailer. "It's got to be five feet long." Randall picked up the stick Michael had used to open the box and lifted the snake.

"Careful," Abby said. "They still have venom in them, even when they're dead."

Randall nodded and glanced around. "Think we should bag it for evidence?"

"Photograph it, then bag it and tag it," Michael said. "The box, too. Maybe we can pick up some prints."

"I doubt it," Randall said. He let the snake drop again. It lay coiled in the dust, still menacing despite its lack of life. "Someone goes to all the trouble to box up a snake and leave it as a present, they're probably smart enough to wear gloves."

"Why would someone do this?" Abby asked.

"They're sending a message." Michael's expression was grim. "Warning you off."

"Warning me off what? I haven't done anything."

"You found that dead man and got us involved," Randall said. "We were close enough to something that sniper fired on us. Maybe they're trying to frighten you out of the backcountry altogether, in case you stumble onto anything else."

"I'm frightened, all right." She shuddered. "I could have been killed."

Michael rested a hand on her shoulder. "You might have been scared half to death. And you'd probably be pretty sick for a while," he said. "But the hospitals around here probably carry antivenin, so chances are good you'd have survived. But whoever did this probably doesn't care one way or another. You're a threat to them, so they're threatening back."

"I haven't done anything to anyone," she protested again.

"You witnessed an execution," he said.

She shuddered at the word. But that was what the murder of that man had been. They'd hunted him down and killed him, like predators hunting prey. "But I didn't see anything. I couldn't identify anyone."

"They can't be sure of that."

"But…how did they know my name?" She shook her head, the reality of what had happened refusing to sink in. "I hardly know anyone in the area—no one who would do anything like this."

"It would be easy enough to learn your name," Randall said. "They could look up your car registration, or get it off your camping permit at the park rangers' office. Using your name makes something like this more personal. More threatening."

She shuddered. She felt threatened, all right. And a little sick.

Michael squeezed her shoulder, then dropped his hand. "You can't stay here," he said.

"No, I can't." This time, whoever hated her had left a snake. What would they do next time? "But where can I go?"

"We'll find you a hotel in town," Randall said. "Register you under an assumed name. One of us can stay with you."

"One of you?"

"I'll stay with you," Michael said.

"You don't have to do that." She straightened her shoulders. "I have a weapon, and I know enough to be careful now. I can look after myself." She'd fought so hard to be independent. She couldn't let this faceless stranger or strangers take that from her.

Michael set his mouth in the stubborn line she was beginning to recognize. "Until we determine how big a threat these people are, I'm going to stay with you," he said.

"I don't need a babysitter." She especially didn't need him hovering. Just because he'd saved her life once didn't mean he was responsible for her the rest of her life. Now that the shock of what had happened was starting to fade, she could think more clearly. "Like you said, this was a warning. If someone had really wanted to hurt me, they wouldn't have bothered gift-wrapping the snake—they'd have turned it loose inside the car." She shuddered at the idea.

"I'm not going to give them a chance to get that close

again." His dark eyes met hers, their previous warmth replaced by cold determination.

"You might as well give up," Randall said. "He's stubborn."

"Fine," she said. "But I'm not sharing a room with you." Having him that close, that…intimate…would be too much.

"I can get a room next door to yours."

"All right." She'd have to learn to live with that.

Randall pulled out a camera and began taking pictures. "Let me see that box," he said. "Maybe Lotte can pick up a scent trail."

But the dog found nothing. Abby went into the trailer to pack while the two officers collected evidence and disposed of the snake. She came out with a suitcase in one hand, her laptop bag and purse in the other, her backpack on her back. "All right, I'm ready," she said. "But in the morning, can I still go out on patrol with you?"

"If you still want to." He took the suitcase from her.

"I want to. Working is better than sitting around brooding about the fact that someone I don't even know hates me enough to attack me with a snake. Besides, I have a lot of territory to cover and only a few weeks to do it. I can't let a threat from a stranger stop me."

MICHAEL TOLD HIMSELF he shouldn't have been surprised by Abby's toughness. She'd already proved she was a survivor. He glanced at her as they negotiated the winding road that led away from the park. The afternoon sun slanted across her face like a spotlight, glinting on the silver earrings she wore. She definitely looked like a beauty queen, or a movie star. "Can I ask you a personal question?"

She turned toward him, her dark blue eyes wary. "You can ask. I don't promise I'll answer."

He focused on the road again. "What happened after you came back to the States—after you were wounded?" he asked. "I mean, how long were you in the hospital? Did you have any kind of rehab, or did they just send you home?"

"I went to a hospital in Germany first. They did surgery there to remove shrapnel, and the surgeons saved my eye. They had to repair my broken cheek." She touched the scar. "I have a titanium plate holding everything together."

He winced. "Sounds brutal."

"I guess it was, but I was in a fog a lot of the time—partly from the drugs, partly from the trauma itself."

"I think that's a protective mechanism the mind has—blocking out trauma that way." In his PJ training, he'd been taught that the wounded seldom remembered what happened on the helicopters.

"I guess, but it bothers me sometimes that I can't remember," she said. "After I was transferred back to the States, to a hospital in Milwaukee, people came to see me and I have no memory of it. And yet the silliest things stay with me."

"Like what?"

"Like I remember I asked my mom to bring me some clothes to wear besides the hospital gown—sweats and things like that. She brought me this yellow blouse I'd always hated. I yelled at her for bringing it and she started to cry. My dad yelled at me for hurting her feelings and then *I* started to cry." She shook her head. "It was just so stupid—what did it matter what color the blouse was?"

"I don't know if it's so stupid," he said. "It makes sense to me. There were so many things happening to you that you couldn't control. The clothes you wore were one little thing you could control. And the medications, not to mention the brain injury, probably made it more difficult to manage your emotions. Your doctors should have told your parents that."

"They probably did. But my mom and dad's way of coping with this whole mess was to pretend nothing was wrong. We'd have these surreal conversations, where Mom would talk about boys I used to date who would be so glad to see me again, and Dad would tell me I should try out for a summer job with the community theater group. After a while, I couldn't stand it anymore and I'd say something horrible, like no one wanted a freak on stage. Then Mom would start to cry again. It was awful."

His hands tightened on the steering wheel. "You're not a freak, you know."

"I know. But I'm not who I was. I'm still coming to terms with that. I don't even want that old life anymore—I'm not sure I ever wanted it. But I'm still figuring out what my new life will look like." She shifted in the seat. "But right now, I'm more focused on figuring out where I'm going to be staying tonight."

"Carmen made reservations at a motel on the other side of town. We figured the farther from the park, the better."

The motel turned out to be one of those old-fashioned lodges with rooms lined up in two low-slung wings on either side of the A-frame lobby. "We have reservations for Ricky and Lucy," Michael told the desk clerk, a fleshy older man with skin the color of raw dough.

He handed over the keys and accepted Michael's credit card, then they drove down to a room on the end and parked. "Ricky and Lucy?" Abby asked. "Why those names?"

"Ricky and Lucy Ricardo? From *I Love Lucy*. I love those old shows. When I had to come up with a couple's names, that popped into my head."

His reply made her feel a little off balance—as if he really was a mind reader. "I love those old shows, too," she said. "When I was in the hospital, I watched a lot of them." Lucille Ball had been a beauty queen who wasn't afraid to make a fool of herself to get a laugh. Watching her had given Abby hope; maybe she could be more than a pretty face herself. But how could Michael know that?

He unlocked the door to the room next to the one on the end and did a quick tour of the space, then looked into the bathroom and checked out the closet. "What are you searching for?" she asked.

"Any sign that anyone's been here ahead of us."

"Why would they have been?"

"Someone might have heard about our plans to stay here. It's not likely, but it pays to be careful."

He unlocked the door to the adjoining room on the end of this wing. "Just to make it easier to reach each other in an emergency," he explained. "You can stay in this room. I'll take the one next door."

His room was a copy of hers, right down to the blue-and-green quilted spread and the bottle of water on the dresser. "What now?" she asked.

"Want to order pizza?"

She almost laughed. After everything that had

happened today, pizza seemed so ordinary. So safe. "That sounds like a good idea."

He pulled out his phone. "What do you like?"

"Anything but anchovies and onions."

He made a face. "Right."

She returned to her room and arranged her few things on the bed and table, then combed her hair and splashed water on her face. She hadn't bothered to do more than apply sunscreen this morning and it showed, her brows and lashes pale and unadorned. She thought about putting on makeup, but she didn't want Michael to get the wrong idea. Circumstances had thrown them together, but it wasn't as if they were dating or anything.

If she was ready to be in a relationship, he wouldn't be her first choice. She was glad he was with her now, and that men like him were hunting down whoever had killed the man in the desert, but he was too intense. Too protective. All his talk of fate and seeing meaning in random happenings unsettled her.

She booted up her laptop and tried to focus on the notes she'd made about desert parsley and its habitat. But that only made her think of Mariposa. She pulled out her phone and studied the picture of the beautiful young woman. Where was she right now? Were she and Angelique safe?

When Michael knocked on the door between their rooms and announced that the pizza had arrived, she gratefully shut down the computer and joined him in his room. The smell of spicy pepperoni and sausage, sauce and cheese made her a little dizzy, and she realized she was starving. "This was a great idea," she said, helping herself to a slice.

"Just what the doctor ordered." He filled his own

plate and sat across from her at the little table in front of the window. He'd drawn the drapes, shutting out the setting sun, and turned on the too-dim lamp behind him. The interior felt cool and cozy.

"Speaking of doctors," she said, "you seem to know a lot about medicine. Did you consider becoming a doctor?"

"Early on, I thought about it. That's why I signed up for the PJs. I thought I wanted a career in trauma medicine. I pictured excitement and the adrenaline rush and saving people's lives." He fell silent and picked a slice of pepperoni off his pizza.

"What is it?" she asked. "Is something wrong?"

"They don't tell you that you lose more than you save." He looked into her eyes. "You were my first save—that's another reason I remember you."

She wanted to look away from the intensity of his gaze, but she couldn't. This man had saved her life; she couldn't turn away from him. "I wish I remembered you," she said. If she did, would she feel that connection between them that he seemed to feel?

He shrugged his shoulders, as if shrugging off bad memories. "Anyway, by the time my tour was up, I'd decided I wasn't cut out for that line of work. I bummed around for a few months, not sure what I wanted to do. After the constant adrenaline rush of the war, civilian life was an adjustment. When my uncle suggested border patrol, I figured I'd give it a shot."

"Do you like it?"

"I like working outdoors, doing something different all the time. I'm not so crazy about the bureaucracy. And sometimes I question whether I'm really doing much good."

"You saved me from that snake." She smiled, letting him know she was teasing.

"If I hadn't gotten to it, Randall would have shot it." He took another bite of pizza and chewed, then swallowed. "Or you'd have killed it yourself. You're tough."

The words made her feel lighter—taller. She smiled. "You couldn't give me a better compliment."

"Is that all it takes?" He grinned, his teeth very white against his olive skin. "Maybe I'll try that line out on other women. I've been doing it all wrong, telling them they were pretty. Not that you aren't—pretty, that is."

Her smile faded. "I heard how pretty I was my whole life. And then I woke up and that was gone. At least something like toughness can't be taken away so easily."

"You talk as though you're horribly disfigured. It's one scar. With your hair down or in profile, it isn't even visible."

"I know it's there, and that affects the way I think about it. I can't help it. I'm not complaining, it's just my reality now."

"Well, just so you know, I think you're beautiful."

"You just admitted you say that to all the girls."

He was about to reply when his phone rang. He set down his slice of pizza and answered it. "Dance."

"Hey, you and Abby get settled in?" Randall's voice was hearty, audible from where she sat.

"We're fine. What's up?"

"I took that snake by the park rangers' office and let them have a look at it," he said. "One of the guys there is a wildlife biologist. He told me something interesting about it."

"Hang on a minute, I'm going to put you on speaker."

Michael glanced at Abby. "It's Randall. He found out something about your snake."

"It's not my snake." She made a face.

"Okay, go ahead," Michael told Randall.

"The snake you killed was a western diamondback," Randall said. "A common desert species, one responsible for most of the deaths from rattlesnake bites in the United States and Mexico."

Michael's eyes met hers across the table. She hugged her arms around herself, her appetite gone. "Why is that so interesting?" he asked.

"They don't have diamondbacks at this elevation," Randall said. "They don't have them at any elevation in Colorado. The only rattlesnakes around her are prairie rattlers—smaller and not as venomous as the diamondback. Whoever boxed up that fellow imported him from somewhere south or west of here."

Michael frowned. "Could you buy something like that at a pet store—you know, one that sells pythons and tarantulas and stuff?"

"It's against the law to sell venomous snakes. No, somebody caught this one in the wild and was keeping it around for special purposes."

"That's sick," Abby said.

"I heard about a drug dealer in Tucson who kept his stash in an aquarium with a venomous snake," Randall said. "It discouraged theft."

Michael sat back in his chair, legs stretched out in front of him. "So what do you make of this?"

"It tells us something about the people we're after," Randall said.

"Yeah, they're twisted."

"Twisted, and they won't stop at anything to protect what's theirs—or to make a point."

"Yeah, well, thanks for the information. I'll talk to you later."

"I'll let you know if anything new develops."

"Yeah. Do that." He hung up the phone and stuffed it back into the pouch on his utility belt.

"What point are they making with me?" Abby asked.

"You must have gotten way too close to something they want very much to hide," he said. "First the sniper, then the snake."

"What are we going to do about it?" She wasn't going to sit here, waiting to be a target.

"Tomorrow, I want to go back out to where we found the body and look around some more."

"I want to come with you."

He shook his head. "I know I said you could go on patrol with me, but this probably isn't safe."

"I've been in unsafe situations before. I want to go. I want to see if we can help Mariposa and her baby."

He paused, considering.

"You said I was tough," she said. "I won't hold you back or get in the way. And if these people are as dangerous as they seem, you shouldn't be out there alone. I can watch your back."

"All right. If I told you no, you'd probably follow me anyway."

"I probably would."

"At least this way I can keep you close, and maybe a little safer."

She started to protest that she didn't need him to protect her, but the words died in her throat. So far, she had needed him. The idea wasn't as disturbing now as it had been earlier. Maybe leaning on someone for help wasn't so bad—if it was the right someone.

Chapter Seven

Belted into the passenger seat of Michael's Cruiser, Abby couldn't shake the feeling that she was headed out on a mission, just like the missions in Afghanistan. The darkness here was like the darkness over there, deepest black, unsullied by the lights of houses or businesses. The nearest city, Montrose, was a dim glow on the horizon.

She leaned forward, straining against the seat belt, trying to see farther into the blackness. Her heart pounded and her nerves twitched with the same jumpy anticipation that had defined every trip she'd made off base during the war. They'd often left early in the morning, to take advantage of the cover of darkness. But their enemies had favored darkness, too, which had made every expedition fraught with danger.

The Cruiser's headlights cut narrow cones into the blackness, enough to illuminate the scraggly trees, jutting rocks and grasses of the park's backcountry. Once, a pair of silvery eyes looked back at them, and as they drew closer, a coyote stared at them, frozen against a backdrop of reddish rocks.

She shivered and pulled her jacket more tightly

around her. Even in summer, it was chilly at this altitude without the sun's warmth.

"You okay?" Michael asked.

"I'm fine." She slipped her hand into her pocket and rubbed her fingers across the little ceramic rabbit. Maybe it was silly for a grown woman to put faith in a good-luck charm, but the rabbit had gotten her through a lot of tough times since her injury. She wasn't ready to give up on it yet.

Michael leaned forward and switched the Cruiser's heat to high. "Tell me more about the research you're doing," he said. "What happens after you gather all these plants and leave here?"

"I'll take them to the lab and experiment with distilling certain compounds from them, and show the effect of those compounds on cells. For instance, if something inhibits cell mutation, it could help fight cancer, or if a substance encourages nerve cells to regenerate, or nerves to build new pathways, it could combat diseases like Parkinson's. I'll have to narrow my research to a single possibility for now, but the prospects for the future are endless."

"That's exciting, that you could be helping so many people. I'd like to do something like that."

She didn't miss the regret in his voice. "You're protecting people from danger," she said. "Making the park safer for visitors, trying to capture people who are hurting others."

"In theory I'm doing those things," he said. "But so far I haven't seen that anything I've done has directly made anyone's life better."

"Except mine," she said. "I wouldn't be here today if it wasn't for you."

He reached across the seat and took her hand and squeezed it. "Yeah. I'm glad about that."

She held his hand for a moment, letting the warmth and reassurance of his touch seep into her. But she couldn't let sentiment overwhelm common sense. Michael Dance was a good guy, but she scarcely knew him. He wasn't a knight in shining armor, and she definitely wasn't a princess who needed rescuing. She pulled away and focused her gaze out the windshield, on the faint band of gray on the horizon. "The sun will be up soon," she said.

If her sudden coolness caught him off guard, he didn't show it. "Check the GPS," he said. "We should be getting close."

She leaned over to glance at the dash-mounted GPS unit. "Looks like maybe another two miles."

"I'm going to cut the lights," he said. "Just in case anyone's watching." He switched off the headlights, plunging them into a disorienting void. She blinked, then he pressed a button and a dim glow illuminated the few inches of ground in front of the Cruiser's bumper. "Sneak lights," he said. "Mounted under the bumper."

She laughed nervously. "Good name."

The Cruiser crawled across the landscape. They'd left the road and followed what was little more than an animal trail—maybe even the same path Abby had followed when she was searching for specimens for her research.

Suddenly, Michael slammed on the brakes. She lurched forward against the shoulder harness. "What's wrong?" she whispered.

"I saw something out there. Movement." He waited a moment and she squinted, trying to make out anything. Though the eastern sky showed a faint blush of pink, it was impossible to make out details in the dim light. "Over there." He pointed up ahead and to the left. He eased his foot off the brake and angled the Cruiser in that direction, and turned on the headlights again. An animal ran in front of the vehicle, and then another.

"Coyotes," she said, and breathed a sigh of relief.

"They're feeding on something." His expression darkened. "We'd better check it out."

"Why? I mean, it's just a bunch of coyotes."

"They're scavengers. They eat whatever they find. For that many of them to be in one place, it must be something good-size."

Her stomach lurched and she swallowed past the sudden bitter taste in her mouth. "Like a body?"

He stopped the vehicle again and turned to her. "I have to check this out, but you can stay in the truck."

"Do you think it's another illegal, like the man we found day before yesterday?" she asked.

"It may not even be a person." The Cruiser rolled forward again.

"But you think it might be."

"It could be. But maybe not an illegal."

"Who, then?"

"A woman went missing in the park a few days ago. At least, she's missing and they found her car abandoned at one of the overlooks. She's a news anchor from a station in Denver—Lauren Starling."

The name sounded vaguely familiar, but Abby couldn't put a face with it. "What would she be doing way out here?" She looked toward the spot ahead where one lone coyote stood guard, his eyes glittering in the Cruiser's headlights.

"She might have stumbled into something she shouldn't have," he said.

The way Abby herself almost had. "I hope not," she said.

"She also might not be connected to this case at all," Michael said. "Some people see the park as a good place to take their own life."

"Suicide? But why in a park?"

"Maybe they think it will be easier on their families, not having to clean up the mess." He braked again, and the lone coyote trotted off. In the glow of the headlights she could make out a brown shape on the ground. There was definitely something there. Her stomach roiled again, and she gritted her teeth against a wave of nausea.

Michael shifted into Park and unfastened his seat belt. "Stay here," he said.

He didn't have to tell her twice. As soon as he opened the door she caught the scent of decay. Of death. She looked away, out the side window, but felt her gaze pulled back to him as he made his way to the formless shape on the ground. He stepped cautiously, his shoulders tensed, one hand on the weapon at his side.

Then he stopped and relaxed. He crouched down and studied the scene a moment longer, then stood and hurried back to the Cruiser. "It's a deer," he said. "There's not enough left to tell how it died. It could have been poachers, or maybe the coyotes managed to separate one from the herd."

She sagged against the seat, weak with relief. "A deer," she repeated. "I was so afraid…"

"I should have just checked it out and not said anything to upset you." He put the Cruiser into gear and turned back toward the track they'd been following.

"I'd have been more upset if you'd clammed up and refused to tell me anything," she said.

"I figured I could count on you to keep a cool head," he said. "I'm not sure how many other civilians would hold it together as well as you have, considering all that has happened."

Since coming to the park she'd stumbled over a dead body and been shot at by a sniper and threatened with a deadly rattlesnake. "I'm not exactly sleeping like a baby, but I'm okay," she said. "Maybe it's similar to being in battle—you do what you have to do at the time, then fall apart later."

He glanced at her. "I hope you don't fall apart."

"Maybe I'm stronger now." Despite a few flashbacks, she did feel stronger. Maybe the man beside her even had something to do with that.

"Give me the GPS coordinates on this spot." He took a small notebook from his shirt pocket.

She read off the coordinates. "Why do you need them?"

He shrugged. "You never know when someone might want to check this out. Maybe we suddenly have a rash of poaching and we need to document it."

"And to think I always pictured national parks as such peaceful, safe places."

"For most people, they are."

She stared out the windshield, at the expanding glow on the horizon. The gray light allowed her to make out more details in the landscape now—the silhouettes of trees and the distant mountains. "We're only a mile or so from the place where the sniper ambushed us," she said.

"I'm going to cut the lights again," he said. "It's getting light enough to see to drive, and if someone's watching, they'll have a harder time spotting us."

She watched the GPS as they crawled forward again. After a few more minutes, she held up her hand. "This is where I parked to hike into the area where we found the body, and where I saw Mariposa."

"And where the sniper fired at us." He put the Cruiser into four-wheel drive and turned off the faint track. "We'll drive a little farther into the backcountry, then get out and have a look around."

She pulled the zipper of her jacket up higher. "What exactly are we looking for?"

"Anything that looks out of place. They'll probably have used camouflage, but a building is tough to conceal. Look for a grouping of trees or rocks that stand out from the rest. Or they could set up a compound in a gully or canyon, where it's harder to detect." He tapped the console between them. "In here is a topo map. I highlighted some places they might try to conceal an operation. There's a Mini Maglite in there, too."

She found the map and light and when he stopped the vehicle she spread the heavy plastic-coated map between them. Yellow highlighter circled a box canyon, a dry wash and a small woodland. She studied the lines indicating elevation. "This wash is closest," she said, pointing to the area he'd circled. "And there's a seasonal creek nearby. This time of year, it will still have water from snowmelt. If I was going to set up a compound out here, that's what I'd choose."

"Let's give it a look, then."

She read out the GPS coordinates, and he turned the Cruiser toward them. "What do we do if we find something?" she asked.

"We call for backup. There's no sense going in alone when we don't even know how many people we're up against. This morning, we're just out sightseeing."

"I'm glad to hear it."

"But you were prepared to go in with just me?" He glanced at her, though she couldn't read his expression in the shadowed interior of the vehicle.

"I guess I trust your judgment," she said. "Is that a mistake?" After all, he didn't strike her as reckless. And he'd saved her life before—she couldn't imagine he'd be eager to throw it away now.

"You can trust me," he said. "Just like I trust you."

"Trust me how?"

"If we do get in a tight spot, I trust you to have my back."

"Of course." The words were casual, but the feeling in her chest was anything but lighthearted. Even the soldiers she'd worked with in Afghanistan weren't all so willing to rely on a woman for help. Michael's high opinion of her meant more than she was ready to say.

"What's that?" He hit the brake and leaned forward, gripping the steering wheel.

"What's what?" She saw nothing in the grayness ahead.

"I thought I saw a light." He switched off the sneak lights and the interior instrument lights. She stared out the windshield at a landscape of gray smudges, backlit by the first rays of the rising sun to their left. But she didn't see the light that had made him stop.

Michael opened the car door. "We better go in on foot," he said. "Stay close to me."

She slipped on her backpack and put one hand to the reassuring heft of the gun at her side. She was back on patrol again, minus the heavier pack and body armor. Even after so much time, the absence of that familiar weight made her feel vulnerable. Exposed.

She shut the door of the Cruiser without making a sound. But there was no way to move across the rugged ground without the occasional scrape of a shoe on rock, or the snapping of a twig that sounded as loud as a slamming door to her ears. Every sense felt heightened—sounds louder, sights clearer, the dawn breeze on her cheeks and the backs of her hands colder. She sniffed the air and grabbed Michael's arm. "Stop."

He halted. "What is it?"

"Do you smell that?"

He inhaled sharply through his nose. "Wood smoke."

"A campfire," she whispered. "I think we're getting very close."

"Which direction do you think it's coming from?"

She considered the question, then pointed ahead and to the right. "Over there."

They moved forward silently, slowly. The sky changed from gray to dusky pink to pale blue. The smell of wood smoke grew stronger, too, and with it came the scent of food—corn, maybe, or baking bread. Soon they were close enough to hear muffled voices, and the scrape of cutlery and clink of glassware.

Michael dropped to his belly and indicated she should do the same. They crawled on their stomachs, dragging themselves forward on elbows. She winced as a sharp rock dug into her forearm. At least here they didn't have to worry about land mines. Probably. She wished she hadn't thought of mines. Someone who'd employ a sniper, and maybe had access to a ghillie suit and military-grade weapons, might decide to use land mines, too.

She started to suggest as much to Michael when they moved around a clump of bushes and suddenly the whole camp was laid out in front of them, tucked into a wash, the depression deep enough so that the surrounding stunted piñons provided cover. Whoever had built the compound had piled brush between the trees to act as a privacy fence. They'd even pulled camouflage netting over the tops of the buildings, making the compound more difficult to detect from the air.

The camp itself wasn't impressive—four old camping trailers in a semicircle around a campfire ring and three warped wooden picnic tables. A brown tarp stretched between poles formed a crude shelter over the tables, where a dozen men and women sat, eating a breakfast of tortillas and beans.

A woman worked at the fire, baking more tortillas on a piece of tin balanced over the coals. When she turned to deliver a fresh batch of the flatbreads to another woman, Abby pinched Michael's arm. "That's Mariposa," she said. She wore the same plaid shawl she'd had on the other day, the baby wrapped securely in its folds.

Michael rose to squat on his heels and indicated they should leave. Reluctantly, she turned to go. She would have liked to talk to Mariposa again, to make sure she was all right. But staying here wasn't safe.

But as they prepared to emerge from the screen of bushes into more open ground, headlights suddenly cut through the darkness. Michael jerked her back into the underbrush and they crouched there, breathing hard and watching a truck make its way toward them.

The truck was bigger than a pickup, with a canvas-covered bed, similar to ones sometimes used by the military to transport troops. It lumbered into camp and stopped not far from the picnic tables. Abby and Michael crept to the edge of the brush once more and watched as two men, carrying semiautomatic rifles, climbed out and spoke to the men and women around the table in Spanish. But they were too far away to make out exactly what they were saying.

Suddenly, the camp sprang to life. The two men with rifles began directing the others to load the picnic tables into the back of the truck. A second truck arrived, and then a third. One man, who wore a white shirt and white straw cowboy hat, and who seemed to be in charge, picked up a bucket and thrust it at Mariposa. She spoke to him, clearly agitated, but he shoved the bucket into her hand and gave her a push. She turned and started walked toward the edge of the compound.

"He told her to get some water and put out the fire," Michael whispered. "They're ordering everyone to load the trucks and prepare to leave."

"I'm going around to the creek to see if I can talk to her and find out more."

Before he could stop her, she was on her feet, headed for the little creek that gurgled a few dozen yards from the camp. She moved cautiously, keeping the screen of brush between her and the activity in the camp. By the time she reached the water, Mariposa was already there, squatting on the bank and dipping the bucket in the shallows.

"Mariposa!" Abby called softly.

The woman looked up, startled. She dropped the bucket and it rolled away, under some bushes.

"Don't run. It's me." Abby moved closer, so the other woman could see her clearly.

Mariposa's expression changed to one of alarm. She spoke softly in rapid Spanish. The only word Abby could make out was *peligroso*—dangerous.

"I want to help you." Why couldn't Abby remember the word for help? She slipped off her pack and started looking for her phone. If she could get a signal out here, she could use a translator on the web to get her message across.

The shouting from camp grew louder. Mariposa glanced over her shoulder, then stood, the bucket abandoned in the creek.

Abby gave up the search for her phone. She dropped the pack and stood, also. "Come with me." She held out her hand. "I can help you."

Mariposa shook her head and started to back away. "No," she said—a word whose meaning was the same in Spanish and English.

"Por favor," Abby said. "Please."

Mariposa looked back toward camp. The shouting sounded closer now. She clutched the baby to her, and Abby was sure she was about to turn and run.

But instead, she untied the shawl and thrust it—and the baby—into Abby's arms. Then she whirled and fled, back toward camp.

Abby stared, stunned, the unfamiliar weight and warmth of the infant in her hands. The child stirred and whimpered, and Abby felt a primal response, a fierce desire to keep this tiny, helpless life safe. She cradled the child to her chest and turned to go back to Michael.

She collided with him just as she turned. For a second they were frozen, his arms steadying her, the baby cradled between them. She fought the instinct to lean into him, to draw strength and comfort from his solid presence. "What happened?" he asked.

"I saw Mariposa. I talked to her. But we couldn't understand each other. I don't know enough Spanish and she doesn't speak English. I think she told me it was dangerous for me to be here."

"She's right. We have to get out of here. They brought another truck in and they're breaking down the camp. We have to get back to the Cruiser and radio for help." He looked down at the bundle in her arms. "What is that?"

"This is Mariposa's baby." She folded back the shawl to reveal the infant's face. The child stared up at them with solemn brown eyes. "Angelique. Mariposa handed her to me, then she ran away. I think she wanted me to keep her safe."

"Come on, we've got to go." He put his arm around her and urged her forward.

They only traveled a few yards before they spotted the line of men and trucks in between them and the Cruiser. Michael swore under his breath. "We'd better risk a call for backup," he said. Huddled in the meager cover at the edge of the woods, he took out first his radio, then his cell. He swore under his breath. "The radio doesn't work this far out, and my phone can't get a signal," he said. "Try yours."

Abby felt sick to her stomach. "My phone is in my

pack, back there by the stream. I was so busy with the baby…"

"I'll get it." He started toward the creek once more, but just then a man stepped out in front of him and leveled a rifle at them. He wore a white shirt, a white hat and a menacing expression.

"You're in the wrong place, amigo," he said.

Chapter Eight

"Abby, run!" Michael shouted.

The last thing she wanted to do was abandon him to the man with the gun, but instinct compelled her to protect the child in her arms. Propelled by the urgency in Michael's voice, she turned and fled, running hunched over to shield the baby, darting and weaving, waiting for the gunshots she was sure would follow. She had no idea where she was headed, but every instinct told her she had to put as much distance as possible between herself and the camp. She could hide in the underbrush and wait until her pursuers were gone.

As for Michael, she prayed he'd find some way to escape. If she could think of any way to come back and help him without endangering the baby, she would.

She stumbled over rocks and brush, her lungs burning. The baby never made a sound. In her short life was she already so familiar with fear and flight? She ran until she was gasping for breath, fighting a painful stitch in her side. The infant was heavier than she looked. Abby stumbled and feared she might drop the child. She'd have to stop and rest for a moment. She needed to get her bearings and figure out her next move.

She huddled behind a pile of rocks, letting her breathing return to normal and her pounding heart slow its frantic racing. The rocks still held the chill of the evening, and she pressed her back against a boulder, letting the coolness seep into her and dry her sweat. She strained to hear any hint of approaching danger. She hadn't heard any gunshots from the camp, but would she have even noticed in her panic to escape?

She peered out from behind the rocks. No one appeared to be coming after her. She couldn't even make out the camp from this distance, but she could see the trucks on the edge of the wash and the bustle of activity around them. If only she had a pair of binoculars.

She needed to get to the truck. Michael probably had supplies and tools in there, maybe even a spare radio. If she could figure out how to start the vehicle, she could drive back to park headquarters and summon help.

She tried to orient herself. The rising sun had been on their left when they'd parked, and they'd walked straight ahead—south. She squinted in the direction she thought the Cruiser should be, but saw nothing. Michael had made a point of parking amid a grove of trees. She'd just have to set out walking in that direction and hope her instincts were right.

Cautiously, she moved out of her hiding place. Now that the sun was fully up, she felt exposed and more vulnerable than ever. But she'd seen no signs of pursuit. And no signs of Michael. Had the man in the white hat shot him and left his body beside the creek?

She pushed the thought away. She had to focus on Angelique now. She folded back the blanket and studied the child, who stared up at her with solemn brown eyes. She stroked the baby's soft cheek with her little finger and Angelique grasped it, holding on tightly. A wave of emotion rose up from deep inside Abby—a fierce protectiveness, longing and love. She would do whatever she had to in order to keep this child safe.

Keeping to the shelter of rocks and trees, she started moving north, on a trajectory she hoped would take her to the parked Cruiser but be well out of the way of the men at the camp. Every few yards she looked back toward the camp, but no one sounded an alarm that they had noticed her.

When she was confident she was well out of sight and sound of the camp, she increased her pace to a ragged trot over the rough ground. With the sun up it was getting warmer, and she wished she'd had some way to collect water back at the creek. If she didn't find the truck, she and Angelique were going to be in trouble.

She stopped to rest a moment and look around. Still no sign of the truck. She should have reached it by now. She couldn't see the camp, either, which made her uneasy. She wanted to be away from it, but she didn't want to accidentally stumble back onto it. She'd read that people who wandered off marked trails in the wilderness tended to walk in circles. Without a map or compass to guide her, she might be doing the same.

A movement somewhere to her right made her freeze. Slowly, she turned her head. Yes, there it was again, a subtle shifting of the brush. A shadow where a shadow shouldn't be. She wrapped her hand around the grip of the Sig Sauer and worked on controlling her breathing. A deep breath in...let it out slowly. She wouldn't shoot unless she had to, but if whoever was out there came too close... She clutched the baby tightly and slid the gun from the holster.

"Abby! Abby, it's me!"

She leaned forward and stared at the man loping toward her. Michael covered the distance quickly, with no sign of injury. She took a few steps toward him, only her grip on the pistol and the baby in her arms keeping her from greeting him with a hug. "How did you get away?" she asked when he stopped beside her.

He bent over, a rifle clutched in both hands, gasping for breath. A moment passed before he could speak, and in that moment she searched for any sign of injury, but he seemed whole and healthy.

He straightened. "When I shouted at you, it distracted the guy enough I was able to kick the gun out of his hands. We struggled for a bit, but I got away."

She nodded to the weapon he was holding. "With the gun."

He hefted the weapon. "He's probably not very happy about that, but I didn't give him any choice."

She glanced over his shoulder at the empty desert. "Are they coming after us?"

"I don't think so," he said. "Not right now anyway. They seemed pretty anxious to clear out." He nodded to the bundle in her arms. "How's the baby?"

"Good. She's very quiet. I'm not sure if that's a good thing or not." She adjusted the blanket to shield Angelique from the sun. "I was trying to get back to the Cruiser," she said.

"Good idea. But first, I want to get a closer look at their trucks before they leave." He turned back toward the camp.

"Wait." She grabbed his arm. "You can't go back there."

"I want to get pictures before they leave—of the

trucks and the people." He pulled his phone from his utility belt. "I can't get a signal, but the camera still works."

"It's too dangerous," she said.

"They won't expect me to come back. You can wait here with the baby."

"No, I'm coming with you." The two of them together, both armed, seemed a better idea than splitting up and forming separate targets. He might think no one was after them, but how could he be sure?

He didn't argue. "We'll follow the creek back to the camp," he said. "The trees will provide cover. We'll keep low and out of sight and just watch and take photographs."

"All right." She didn't like the plan, but she liked being left alone out there less.

They intersected with the creek farther up the wash and followed it down toward the camp. Soon, the slamming of vehicle doors and murmur of voices in Spanish filled the air. Michael stopped about a hundred yards from all the activity and crouched down. She huddled behind him, peering over his shoulder.

The men with guns stood guard as the other men and women filed into the trailers. Abby counted six people filing into one of the campers, which was smaller even than the one she'd rented for the summer. When all the people were inside, the guard reached up and locked the door, then pocketed the key.

"What are they doing?" she whispered, her lips against Michael's ear.

"I think the trucks are going to tow the trailers out of here."

Before he had even finished speaking, one of the

trucks had backed up to the trailer and begun the process of hooking on to the camper. Michael pulled out his camera and snapped picture after picture. Abby searched the camp for any sign of Mariposa, but couldn't find her. Was she already locked into one of the crowded trailers?

The man in the white shirt and hat who'd confronted them by the creek stood to one side. He'd found another rifle and held it across his chest, barking orders at the others. Within a quarter of an hour, the camp was clear. The man in the white shirt surveyed the area and seemed satisfied. He climbed into the vehicle at the front of the line and the trucks—four of them now, each with a trailer in tow—pulled away from the campsite. Two set out toward the main road, while the other two started cross-country.

When the vehicles were too far away for anyone to see them, Michael crawled out of their hiding place and stood to get a better look. "Where are they going?" Abby asked.

"There are a lot of old ranch roads and two-tracks cutting across this property. They're probably taking a roundabout way to the highway. My guess is the other two will turn off at some point, too. They won't want to risk being seen on the main park road by one of the park rangers or one of our team."

"What do we do now?" she asked.

"I'd like to get some people out here to comb this place for evidence."

"Are they going to find anything?" Except for an area bare of vegetation where the fire and picnic tables had been, there was little sign of the compound that had been here only an hour before. Even the rocks that had been used to make the fire ring had been cleaned and scattered, the footprints of those who had been here smoothed over with a branch of juniper.

"You never know." He stared at his phone. "Still no signal."

"Maybe mine will work," she said. "Now that they're gone, I can retrieve my pack."

"Good idea. Where is it?"

"Back this way." She led the way along the creek to the spot where she'd talked to Mariposa. She scanned the creek bank. "I don't see it," she said. "I could have sworn it was right in here."

"It was blue, right?"

She nodded. "Bright blue. It shouldn't be hard to spot." She walked along the bank, looking into the water and underbrush, even though she knew she had dropped it in the open. He searched, also.

"One of them must have seen it and taken it," he said. "What was in there besides your phone and the GPS?"

"Water, food, a first-aid kit. A space blanket, another pair of socks, a whistle, compass and fire starter." She ticked off the items in a standard backcountry emergency list—all things they could have used right now.

"They didn't leave anything behind," he said, looking around.

"Except this." She reached under a bush and started to pull out the metal bucket Mariposa had carried to the creek. "Though I don't see what good it's going to do us."

"Don't touch it." His hand on her arm stopped her and he moved up beside her. "We might get good prints off it that could help us identify some of the people involved."

"What should we do with it?" She stepped back.

"Leave it here. We'll want to get a team in here to go over the place—they can pick it up then." He tied his bandanna to a nearby tree branch to mark the spot.

"We just have to find our way back to headquarters," she said. "And find our way here again after that."

He straightened and looked around them, as if studying the terrain—the low hills and more distant mountains. "Which way is the canyon from here?" he asked. "Black Canyon." If they could find the canyon, they'd find the road that led to the headquarters.

"I don't know." She turned slowly in a circle, looking around them. "That's the thing about this place. The canyon isn't something you see from ground level. You have to be right up on it before you know it's there."

"What do we do now?" she asked.

"We can try to find the truck."

Her expression lightened. "I do know which direction the truck was in. All we have to do is walk right through there." She pointed to a cut in the fringe of trees along the edge of the wash, then set off at a brisk pace, Michael close behind her.

After twenty minutes of walking and backtracking, they didn't find the Cruiser. But they did find the tracks where it had been parked, and the tracks of the other vehicles that had passed. "What happened?" she asked.

"They stole it," he said. "Trucks don't just vanish, so one of them must be driving it."

"If they found the truck, they must know we're still out here," she said.

He nodded, his expression grim. "They'll probably send someone back to find us. We need to get out of here before that happens." He pulled out his phone and tried it, but it continued to show no signal. "We need higher ground." He looked around and spotted a low hill. "Up there."

She cradled Angelique in her arms as she climbed up the hill, praying that someone didn't have her in the sights of a rifle's scope as she climbed. She felt too exposed up here on the side of this hill. Anyone who looked in this direction would be able to spot them. She picked up her pace, anxious to find cover once more.

At the top of the rise, she ducked behind a low piñon and struggled to catch her breath. Michael stood a little ways from her, holding up his phone. "I think this is going to work," he said. "I'm getting a signal." He started walking backward, watching the screen, the phone in one hand, the radio in the other. "Almost there."

And then he was gone, dropping over the edge, a cascade of falling rocks and a single startled cry the only indication he had ever been there.

Chapter Nine

Michael scrabbled for a hold on the crumbling shale that continued to give way beneath his feet and slip from his hands. He dropped the phone and the radio—the radio somersaulting into the air and out of sight, the phone bouncing like a thrown rock as it, too, disappeared into the canyon. He kicked out his feet and found only air, and an image of his body, broken and bleeding, at the bottom of the gully flashed through his mind.

Frantic, he hurled himself toward a ragged piñon that jutted from the canyon wall. His fingers grasped the prickly needles, and he swung his other hand up to grip a branch. The tree bent and creaked, but held.

He hung there for a long moment, struggling to breathe and to slow the pounding of his heart. He found a toehold for one foot in the rock below and supported his weight partially on one leg, with the other resting uncomfortably against the slick, steep canyon wall.

He'd fallen about ten feet, though it had seemed farther. His instinct was to shout for help, but he checked it. All of the men from the camp might not have left in the trucks. He didn't know who was up there, looking for him.

And looking for Abby and the baby. He had to keep quiet for their sake.

Just then, Abby's face appeared above him. She was kneeling at the edge of the drainage into which he'd fallen, looking down at him, her forehead creased in a worried frown. "What happened?" she asked, her voice carrying to him in the clear air, though she didn't shout.

"I must have slipped. Stupid move." He should have known to be more careful on this unpredictable terrain, but it was too late to berate himself now.

"Can you climb up?"

He considered the almost vertical wall above him, lined with brittle shale and slick mud. Here and there tufts of grasses or wildflowers clung to the side—feeble handholds for a man who weighed one-eighty. "I don't suppose you have a rope," he said.

"Sorry. I'm fresh out."

"Yeah, I thought so." Already his arms were beginning to feel as if they'd pull out of their sockets. He couldn't hang here much longer. "What's happening up there?" he asked.

"Angelique is fussy—I think she's hungry. I've got her here beside me."

Of course her first concern was for the child. "No sign of the bad guys?"

"No sign of them. What can I do to help?"

"Maybe say a prayer." He focused on a clump of grass three feet overhead. "What do you know about native grasses?" he asked.

"Um, a lot, actually. What do you want to know?"

"Do they have very deep roots?"

"It depends. Some of them have very deep roots. That helps them find scarce water, and also prevents erosion."

And maybe they'd save his life. He took a deep breath, stretched up and took hold of the clump of grass. He lost his toehold and scrabbled for a new one, plastered against the side of the canyon, cool mud against his cheek, the scent of wet earth and sage filling his nostrils.

He clawed at the canyon wall and dug in with fingers, knees, toes—anything to keep from falling. Agonizing inch by agonizing inch, he crept toward the top, muscles screaming, mind fighting panic. Whenever he dared look up, he saw Abby's face, pale against the dark juniper and deep blue sky. Her eyes never left him, the tip of her thumb clenched between her teeth.

Having her there helped some. She gave him a goal to reach, a bigger reason to hang on. She and that baby depended on him to get them out of here safely. Giving up wasn't an option.

The climb to the top seemed to take an eternity, though in reality probably only fifteen minutes or so passed. When he dragged himself over the edge at last, he lay facedown on the ground, spent and aching.

Abby rested her hand on his back, a gentle weight grounding him to the earth and to her. "Are you all right?" she asked.

He pushed up onto his elbows. "Do we have any water?"

"No."

Of course they didn't. They also didn't have a phone or radio or GPS. They had two guns, the energy bar he'd stashed in his jacket, the hard candies he always carried and whatever Abby was carrying in her pockets. They also had a baby, who was going to get hungry sooner rather than later, and no idea where they were.

He sat up and pulled out his bandanna to wipe as much mud as he could from his face and hands. The baby began to whimper and Abby gathered it into her arms and rocked it. He studied her, head bent low over the fussy child, her blond hair falling forward to obscure half her face. She reminded him of a Madonna—a particularly beautiful one.

The memory of the way she'd touched him just now lingered, but he pushed it aside. He had to focus on how they were going to find their way back to headquarters. "Do you know where we are?" he asked.

She jerked her head up. "Don't you?"

He fought the instinct to play the macho man and lie to her, but lies like that only led to trouble. He shook his head. "We arrived in the dark, so I couldn't orient by landmarks. I made the mistake of relying on GPS." He looked around them, hoping to recognize some familiar rock outcropping or group of trees.

She moved up behind him to look over his shoulder. He became aware of her body pressed to his, her warmth seeping into him. "What do we do now?" Her breath tickled the hair at the back of his neck, sending heat sliding through him.

"I'm open to suggestions."

Abby cradled the child to her shoulder and rocked her gently. "We've got to get food for the baby," she said. "And water."

"The creek has water. I can't say how safe it is to drink, but it's a start." His own mouth felt as if he'd been chewing sawdust. He couldn't let dehydration cloud his judgment.

"So we'll walk back to the creek and get water," she said. "Then what?"

"Then I think we'd better sit down to wait."

"Wait for what?"

"For the Rangers to find us—or for whoever is in charge of the camp to return."

"Do you really think they'll come back?"

"They know we're still out here. Without a vehicle, we can't go too far. If they know we have the baby, they'll realize that will slow us down, even if we had a destination in mind. So yeah, I think they'll come back. We're a problem they won't let rest until they take care of it. The trick will be for us to take care of them first." He reached back and took her hand. "Come on."

ABBY'S FEET DRAGGED as she followed Michael back toward the creek and the deserted encampment. She hadn't slept well last night—the vision of the rattlesnake, alive and ready to strike, imprinted on the insides of her eyelids every time she closed them. Up at four this morning, then the tension and adrenaline rush of the events of the day, plus the ground they'd covered on their hikes around the area, had all taken their toll. She was exhausted, and the baby in her arms felt like a twenty-pound bowling ball.

But she could do nothing but keep moving. Going back to wait for the people who wanted them dead seemed foolhardy at best, suicidal even. But the move also made sense. Every survival manual she'd ever read stressed staying in one location if you were lost. Wandering aimlessly complicated the search for you and wasted precious energy. At least by the camp they'd have water, which all needed, but Angelique, especially, had to have.

Michael looked back over his shoulder. "How are you doing?" he asked.

"I'm hanging in there."

"And the baby?"

"She seems to like the movement." She smiled down at the infant, who had fallen asleep. "She must have spent a lot of time moving around with her mother."

"It looked as if Mariposa was in charge of the cooking today. She probably spent a lot of time on her feet, gathering water, cleaning up and cooking the meals."

"What did the other people, the ones we saw eating, do?"

"They probably worked tending a crop of marijuana, or making meth, though I didn't see any signs of production around the trailer, and I didn't smell anything off. So probably marijuana."

"Are they here voluntarily?"

"Probably not. They may have crossed the border looking for work, but once they arrived here, they were prisoners."

"So they're slaves?"

"Pretty much, yeah."

"It…it's like something out of another century. Not something that should happen today in the United States."

"It happens more than people imagine—probably more than the statistics say, though the Justice Department estimates that more than seventeen thousand people a year are brought into the United States for trafficking purposes. They're forced to work in factories or on farms, and as household help. More than eighty percent of trafficking victims are sex slaves. Many of them are immigrants, though young Americans, runaways and homeless teens get caught up in trafficking, too."

"That's appalling."

"It is." He looked toward the now-deserted camp. "If these people are involved in that kind of thing, I want to stop them."

"I want to stop them, too," Abby said. "But we also need to get Angelique to a safe place. She's going to need to eat soon, and she'll need diapers." So many things they didn't have here in the middle of nowhere. Worry settled like a brick in her stomach. "How long do you think it will be before your team realizes we're missing?"

He glanced up at the sky, the color of purest turquoise. "They'll expect me to check in in a few hours, at the latest."

And it would probably be hours after that before anyone became really concerned, she thought. After all, their plan had been to spend the day in the backcountry, where it wasn't unusual to be without cell phone and radio signals. She shifted the baby to her other shoulder. They needed to find a place to settle and wait.

They had to cross a hundred yards of open prairie to reach the first cover that led along the edge of the wash to the creek. The wash itself began as a depression in the landscape, then gradually deepened and widened into the side drainage where Michael had fallen. That mini canyon was only about thirty feet deep—compared to the Black Canyon that gave the park its name, which plunged more than two thousand seven hundred feet at its deepest point.

Michael drew his gun. At least he hadn't lost it in the fall. "How do you feel about making a run for it?"

he asked. "Just in case someone is out there looking for us?"

"Do you really think they left someone behind to search for us?" she asked.

"I don't know. But we shouldn't take chances."

She nodded. "What do you want me to do?"

"Run as fast as you can to that clump of trees over there." He indicated a grouping of scrub oak. "I'll cover you. Then you can do the same for me."

She studied the expanse of ground, with its scant vegetation and rocky surface. "All right." Then she took off, cradling the infant to her, her feet raising little puffs of dust as she zigzagged her way across the ground. Within seconds, she'd reached the safety of the rocks; no one had fired.

He waited until she removed the Sig Saucr from the holster at her right hip and nodded in his direction. His darted out into the open, running hard, pumping his arms and legs, taking long strides, covering the ground as rapidly as possible. Then he threw himself on the ground beside her, too winded to speak.

"You looked good," she said. "Did you ever run track?"

He nodded. "In high school." He wiped his mouth. "A long time ago."

"I never liked running," she said. "Those drills were the worst part of basic training for me."

"I'm still trying to picture a beauty queen in boot camp."

She made a face. "I didn't tell anyone I was a beauty queen. If anything, I tried to make myself as plain as possible—no makeup, hair scraped back into a ponytail."

"I'll bet it didn't work," he said. "No one—no man,

for certain—would ever mistake you for homely." He stood and offered a hand to help her up. "You ready?"

"Ready." She stood, but didn't let go of his hand right away. When their eyes met, she offered a shy smile before turning away and moving toward the creek.

At the creek bank, Michael knelt to drink. Abby wandered along the bank, searching the ground.

He looked up, the cuffs of his sleeves and the front of his shirt damp from the creek water. "What are you looking for?"

"This." She held up a nearly new tin can she'd plucked from beneath a tree. She'd spotted the label earlier and it had vaguely registered as just another piece of garbage—a can that had once held corn and been discarded. "We can make a fire and boil water for Angelique," she explained. "You and I can deal with an upset stomach from anything that might be in that water, but a baby could die from the wrong bacteria."

"Good idea." He stood and pointed up the creek bank. "Let's move to that rock outcropping there. We'll be sheltered a little from the sun and wind, and we'll have a good view of anyone approaching the camp from this direction."

He led the way to a spot beneath a lone piñon that seemed to grow straight out of the surrounding rock. The stunted tree leaned crazily to one side, its branches spread like open arms, casting a pool of shade on the red granite. Michael began gathering pine needles and bark for tinder. "I had fire starters and matches in my pack," she said.

"See if you can find some broken glass around the camp. Otherwise, I can make a fire drill out of two sticks. It takes forever, but it does work."

She returned to the creek to wash out the can and fill it with water. She got a drink for herself and studied the plants that grew in or near the water. Ten minutes later, she returned to camp, feeling triumphant.

"What are you grinning about?" Michael asked.

"I found a good piece of glass." She held up what looked like the bottom of a jar. "And I found these." She opened the sling and began laying out the plants she'd gathered.

He took the glass and studied the plants. "What is all that?"

"Wild lettuce, cress and mustard. Wild onion. A few piñon nuts." She pointed to the various plants. "We can have a salad for lunch."

"If you say so."

"I'll see to the baby first, then I'll prepare some of this for us."

Using the piece of glass to focus sunlight on the tinder, Michael soon had a fire going. He fed the small blaze with more tinder, then twigs, and finally dead wood he'd salvaged from around the camp. Abby balanced the can of water on three rocks in the center of the blaze. When the liquid was boiling, she used the sleeve of her jacket like a potholder to remove it from the heat. "You still have Life Savers with you, don't you?" she asked.

"Sure." He fished the roll from his pocket.

"Let me have a couple."

He handed over the candies and she dropped them in the hot water. "They'll make a kind of sugar water for the baby."

"Clever," Michael said.

"The sugar will give her a little energy," Abby said.

"And the sweet taste might make her more willing to drink." While the water cooled, she set about stripping the stems from leaves and cleaning dirt from roots she collected.

Michael moved closer. "Is all that really edible?" he asked.

"Sure. All our native salad greens started out as wild plants. People think of this as a desert, but there are really a lot of edible plants here, if you know what to look for."

"What can I do to help?" he asked.

He'd already been a big help, keeping her calm and starting the fire. His steady, capable presence reassured her. "Just keep me company while I work. Were you a Boy Scout when you were little?"

"I was. And my family went camping a lot. Every other weekend in the summer, we'd pack the car with a tent and sleeping bags and a cooler and head to the national forest. We'd hike and fish and roast marshmallows around a campfire."

"And you liked that?"

"Are you kidding? For two days, my sister and I had our parents all to ourselves. We ran around outside, ate hot dogs and hamburgers, and no one cared how dirty we got. It was great." He smiled, remembering. "Those trips made me love being outdoors. They're probably why I was attracted to this job."

"You weren't worried you'd end up in an office, reviewing paperwork?"

"There's paperwork in every job, but from the first I applied for positions that allowed me to be out and on my own more. If it weren't for the crime and the bad guys, this would be the ideal job. What about you? Were you a Girl Scout?"

She shook her head. "Oh, no. My mother would not have spent the night outdoors unless forced to do so at gunpoint. I spent my weekends at dance recitals and beauty parlors and pageant practice."

"Boot camp must have been a big culture shock."

"It was and it wasn't." She tested the water in the can. Still a little too warm. "When I was in high school, I joined the school hiking club. It introduced me to a whole new group of kids—kids who liked to camp and hike and spend time outdoors."

"And they accepted you?"

"They were suspicious at first, but after I proved myself, they saw me as one of them. I discovered how much I liked spending time in the woods. A couple of my friends in the club went into the military right out of high school. Later, when I was searching for something to do with my life, I remembered them and thought, 'Why not?'"

She settled back against the trunk of the tree and unfastened the sling, using it as a blanket to swaddle the baby. Angelique fussed and began to cry. "I know, sweetheart. You're probably hungry." She dipped her finger in the can and brought it to the baby's lips. "Let's see if you'll take some of this for me."

The little mouth latched on to her finger and Abby felt a pull deep within her womb. She dribbled more water into the infant's mouth.

"I think she likes it." Michael had moved closer and watched the two of them with his usual intensity.

"At least it will keep her hydrated," she said. "But I hope someone comes for us soon."

"We might have to spend the night out here, but to-morrow, I know someone will come for us," he said.

The idea of a night without shelter, blankets or formula didn't thrill her, but whining about it wouldn't change anything. For now, Angelique seemed content, and that was all that mattered.

"Why do you think Mariposa gave her to you?"

She'd had plenty of time to ponder the answer to that question. "The only reason I can imagine a mother would give up her baby was because she thought Angelique would be safer with me." And Mariposa must have been desperate, to hand her child over to a stranger.

"Why didn't she give the baby to you the first day you two met?"

"Maybe she's learned some new information since then that made her fear for her safety—or the baby's safety."

"Maybe breaking up camp today didn't have anything to do with us finding that dead man," he said. "Maybe something else is up."

"Like what?"

"I don't know. But if she thought the baby was going to be in danger, she would have tried to protect her."

Anger at the thought of anyone trying to hurt this baby pushed away some of her weariness. "I want to find whoever's responsible and make sure they're punished," she said.

"I want to find them, too." He pulled out his phone and clicked over to the photos he'd taken earlier.

"Did you get anything useful?" she asked.

He squinted at the photos of the trucks lined up, ready to leave. "I can't make out the license plates," he said. "I think they've splattered them with mud."

"Who was the man you fought with?" she asked. "Do you have any idea?"

He shook his head. "Mariposa called him El Jefe—the chief. My guess is he's the boss, at least on this level."

"So there's probably someone else supervising operations above him?" she asked.

"Probably. Someone who doesn't get his hands dirty by dealing with people directly. He probably ordered them to move camp, now that we've gotten so close."

"Why didn't they leave yesterday, after the sniper fired at us?" she asked.

"I don't know. Maybe they had to get permission from someone higher up the chain of command. Or maybe they had to wait for the trucks to arrive from somewhere else."

"Yet they still had time to gift wrap a rattlesnake for me."

"If the two incidents are related. We don't know that for sure."

She leaned back against a tree trunk, the baby cradled to her shoulder. "I promise you, no one else hates me enough to send me a deadly snake."

"No jilted lovers or brokenhearted ex-boyfriends?" He kept his tone teasing, but she sensed a tension in the air as he waited for her answer.

"Not a one. I haven't been in any kind of relationship since before I joined the army. And none of them were serious. And please don't insult me with clichés like 'a pretty woman like you' or 'having so much to offer.' I get enough of that from my parents. I've been too busy—first with rehab, now with school—to worry about relationships."

"I wasn't going to say anything."

She shifted toward him. "What about you? Do you have a woman waiting for you back home—wherever home is?" Now it was her turn to hold her breath, waiting for his reply. She didn't like to admit how much his answer mattered to her.

"No. I didn't date a lot, though I always had women friends. The last long-term relationship I had, several years ago, she broke it off because she said I was too intense. I wasn't even sure what she meant."

Yes, he could be intense, a trait that both drew her to him and made her wary. "I think you're the kind of man who, when you do something, you don't give a half measure. You put everything you have into it, whether it's a job or a relationship. If someone else isn't ready for that level of commitment, that can feel too intense. It can be scary."

"Are you scared of me?"

She didn't look away from him, her gaze steady. He'd been honest with her; now it was her turn. "I'm not scared of you, Michael. But fear doesn't always— or even usually—come from other people. More often, we're scared of something inside ourselves. Of our own beliefs or emotions."

"I'm glad you're not afraid of me," he said. "I've got your back, remember?"

A hint of a smile curved her lips. "Yeah. I remember."

Chapter Ten

Michael kept his eyes locked to Abby's, willing her not to look away. What was she scared of inside herself, and how could he help her let go of that fear? But he got the impression if he tried to get that personal, she'd just pull back. As with the fall of hair that kept hiding her scar, Abby liked to keep layers between her and other people.

The baby started fussing, breaking the spell between them. Abby turned away and he sat back, stifling a sigh of frustration.

"I need your bandanna," she said. "The baby's diaper is soaked."

He handed it over, and she folded it into a makeshift diaper and handed him the soaked one. "Wash this out—downstream."

He made a face, but moved off to do as she asked. Washing dirty diapers wasn't on the list of things he had expected to do in this job, but there was something calming and grounding about the mundane, domestic chore. Yes, he was lost in the wilderness with the possibility that a killer was searching for them, but his duty was crystal clear—to protect this woman and this baby and somehow return them to safety.

The man in charge of this camp would be back.

Everything in the man's attitude and posture told Michael he wasn't one to overlook a threat. He'd been outsmarting the Rangers for weeks. The urgency of moving his people might have forced him to delay the hunt momentarily, but he wasn't going to let two people who had discovered his secret get away. When he'd stolen Michael's Cruiser he'd left the couple stranded, so he could be confident they were still close by. As long as Michael saw the man before he spotted them, they'd be safe. He'd make sure of it.

He had Abby to help, too. Thanks to her, they wouldn't starve. Roots and leaves weren't steak and potatoes, but his growling stomach would be thankful for anything he fed it. And being with Abby made him feel calmer and more certain that they'd come through this all right. She was worried, but not panicking. Anyone who mistook her for a dumb blonde was delusional.

He rejoined her and she sat up straighter, her hand making a fist in her lap.

"What do you have there?" He nodded to her fist.

She flushed. "It's nothing."

He spread the damp diaper on a tree branch to dry. "It's not nothing. What is it?"

She looked away. "I've been watching and I haven't seen any sign of anyone headed this way," she said.

Message received. She didn't want to talk about whatever she was holding. "We ought to be able to see the dust from a vehicle from a long way off," he said.

"How far do you think we are from the main road?" she asked.

"About five miles, I think. Maybe a little more."

"Where do you think they were taking those people?"

"To another camp in the park—or maybe all the way to Denver. I don't know."

"What a harsh life." She arranged the shawl to shade the sleeping infant. "Who's behind this?"

He sat beside her, wrists on his upraised knees. "We don't know that, either. There are rumors drug cartels have moved in from Mexico, but they need a local connection—a sponsor who can smooth the way for them."

"Who?"

"That's one of the things we've been trying to find out. It has to be someone with money. Someone powerful. Someone who thinks he's above the law."

"Do you have someone in mind?"

"We do. But we can't prove anything." Though law enforcement might rely on hunches to guide their investigation, they needed proof to stand up in court.

"Tell me. It's not as if I'll tell anyone else."

"Have you heard of a man named Richard Prentice?"

"No. But I'll admit, I've been so busy with school I haven't paid much attention to the news."

"He's a billionaire who owns the land at the entrance to the park."

"The place with the big stone pillars and iron gate?"

"That's the one. He's made a lot of money buying historic or critical wilderness properties and selling them to the government or conservation groups for inflated prices. But the Feds wouldn't bite when he tried to sell that place, and local governments passed restrictions that limited how he could develop it. So he made it his base of operations."

"I suppose it's a good location for overseeing a drug

operation within the park, but why would a guy like that bother with drugs? He's already rich."

"Some people never have enough money. But maybe it's not about the money for him. Maybe this is one more way to stick it to a government he seems to hate. Or maybe he gets a rush out of having control over so many people's lives."

"If he does have anything to do with this, I hope you can prove it and send him to jail for a long time."

"That's what we hope, too."

She shifted onto her knees. "Take the baby for a minute," she said. "I think our food is about ready." Not waiting for an answer, she shoved the infant into his arms.

The baby was heavier than he'd expected, warm and a little wiggly, too. As he tried to figure out the most comfortable way to hold her, she opened her eyes and stared up at him. She seemed so bright and alert, her gaze fixed on him, as if assessing him. "You're onto me, kid," he said softly. "I don't have the faintest idea what I'm doing."

She shifted, curling toward him with a little sigh that made his heart stop for a moment. He stared down at her, gripped by the most intense, protective instinct he'd ever felt. "I won't let them hurt you, little girl." He stroked her cheek with the tip of his finger, the skin softer than anything he'd ever felt.

"She likes you." Abby returned, holding a section of bark like a plate. "She settled right down."

"I don't have a lot of experience with babies."

"You're a natural." She set the "plate" on the ground between them. "I can take her again if you want."

"No. That's okay." The infant fit neatly in the crook

of his left arm, leaving the right arm free. "I don't want to disturb her." He leaned forward to study the items she'd arranged on the bark. "What's on the menu?"

"The salad greens I talked about earlier—no dressing, I'm afraid. The little white things are mariposa lily bulbs I roasted."

He popped one of the buds—about the size of a garlic clove—into his mouth and chewed. "Not bad. A little earthy, but a little sweet, too."

"They'd be better with salt or other seasonings, but they'll keep us going until help arrives."

"Not bad at all." He crunched down on another bulb.

They finished the meal in silence. Hunger sated, with the warmth of the sun off the rocks and the profound silence of the wilderness closing in, his eyelids began to feel heavy. He sat up straighter. He had to stay awake and watch for rescue—or the return of the camp boss.

"I think the early morning and all that hiking is catching up with me," Abby said.

"You can take a nap," he said. "I'll keep watch."

"I might have to." She looked around them. "Not that all this rock is going to make for a comfortable bed."

"Come lean against me." He patted the spot beside him.

She hesitated.

"Come on. I won't bite."

"You'd better not. I bite back." But she settled beside him.

He slipped his arm around her shoulder. "Just lean on me."

Again, she hesitated, but the gentle pressure from his hand coaxed her to lay her head in the hollow of his shoulder. She settled down with a sigh, her breast and side pressed against him, one hand resting on his thigh. He felt the same protective instinct toward her he'd felt toward the baby, but underneath the protectiveness was a more primal emotion, the awareness of her as a beautiful, desirable woman, and of himself as a man who wanted her.

The wanting was nothing new. He'd been physically attracted to her from the moment she walked into ranger headquarters. That in itself wasn't that unusual. He was attracted to women every day, a passing desire akin to seeing a luscious brownie and his mouth watering.

His desire for Abby went deeper. She wasn't a passing fascination. The more he knew her, as a complex, capable, sympathetic person, the more he felt drawn to know her more fully. Intimately.

She shifted against him and he looked down to find her head tipped up toward his. "You wanted to know what I was holding earlier," she said.

"You don't have to tell me if you don't want to," he said. "It's none of my business."

"No—I want to tell you." She held out her fisted hand and slowly opened her fingers to reveal the figure of a leaping rabbit, about three inches long. "It's just a kind of good-luck charm I keep. I know it's silly, but holding it makes me feel calmer."

"It's not silly." He was feeling anything but calm himself right now, but he didn't want to scare her by overreacting. "Do you remember where you got it?"

"I don't know." They both studied the little rabbit in her palm. It was white with brown spots, four legs outstretched as if running, ears erect. "When I came to in the hospital, I was holding it."

"I wasn't sure if you remembered." He could hardly

get the words out past the knot of emotion in his throat. He tried again. "Before they unloaded you off the chopper, I put it in your hand and you grasped it. It seemed like a good sign. Even unconscious, you were fighting. Hanging on."

She stared. He tried to read the emotion in her eyes and drew back a little. She looked upset. Maybe even angry. "Why did you do that?" she asked.

"My cousin gave it to me when I deployed," he said. "She said if one rabbit's foot was supposed to be lucky, she figured four feet, still attached to the rabbit, were even better. I figured you needed the luck more than I did right then."

She wrapped her fingers around the little figure again and returned it to her pocket, not looking at him. "Thank you," she said. "I always wondered where he came from."

"Did it help?"

She nodded. "It did. Whenever I was stressed or worried or needed distracting, I'd take him out and hold him. It reminded me that someone I didn't even know had been rooting for me to make it." She raised her head and looked at him, her eyes glinting with unshed tears. "Now I know that someone was you."

He couldn't speak, afraid of saying the wrong thing. Of breaking the connection between them. She sat up a little straighter, though she remained pressed against him. "I have a hard time warming up to people. Especially since I got home from Afghanistan."

"The things you went through over there—you can't really share them with others. They're like an invisible wall, separating you from everyone else who doesn't know what it's like. They can never see things from your point of view."

"But you can."

"Not entirely. But I have a better idea than some."

"Yes." She put her hand on his chest.

"Do you think that's all we have in common—the war?" He forced himself to look into her eyes, not sure he'd like the answer she gave. He hated the idea that she'd see him as just another damaged veteran with whom she could compare notes.

"I didn't mean it like that," she said. "Only that I felt comfortable enough with you to let my guard down a little. When you look at me, I feel like you see all of me—not just the beauty queen, and not just the scarred veteran, but the whole package."

He touched her cheek with his free hand. "It's a very nice package." He dragged his thumb across the corner of her mouth.

She let out her breath in a soft sigh and leaned closer. That was all the invitation he needed. He bent his head and covered her lips with his own. She returned the kiss, arching into him and sliding her hand around to clutch his shoulder. He wrapped his free arm around her and pulled her to his chest, her soft, feminine curves molding to him. He slanted his mouth more firmly against hers and she parted her lips, her tongue tracing the crease of his mouth, setting his heart racing.

She melded her body to his, urgent, needy. This wasn't a casual, flirtatious kiss, or one of tentative exploration. This kiss spoke of built-up longing, of a craving for a connection that went beyond words.

Angelique squirmed against him and began to whimper. Reluctantly, he broke the kiss and tried to comfort the baby. "I must have been crushing her," he said.

"I'll take her." Head down, hair falling forward to cover the side of her face and shield her expression from his view, she reached for the infant.

He slipped the baby into her arms, unsure of what he should say. Kissing was one thing—talking about it was another. Still, he couldn't let the moment pass as if nothing had happened. He reached out and brushed back her hair. "Are you okay?" he asked.

"I'm fine." She took a deep breath and raised her eyes to meet his. "We probably shouldn't have done that."

"Why not?"

"Because…." She bit her lower lip, then shook her head.

"Tell me." He cradled the side of her neck. "You seemed to be enjoying yourself at the time."

A warm flush crept up her cheeks—all the answer he really needed, but he held back a smile of triumph. "I don't want you to get the wrong idea," she said. "I'm not really ready…for more than kisses. For a relationship."

Her obvious distress touched him. "I'm in no hurry. No pressure, I promise." He sat back again. "If the baby's all right, you can take that nap now. I promise I won't bother you."

After a moment of hesitation, she settled against him once more, the baby wrapped in the sling and fastened around her. He stared out across the empty landscape and listened to the rhythm of her breathing slow and deepen as she fell asleep. At least with her this close, every nerve in his body aware of her, he wasn't too worried about falling asleep himself. He'd stay awake and keep watch, protecting her with his life if he had to.

MICHAEL WOKE WITH a start and stared out at the sun, which was sliding toward the horizon, the intense heat of midday fading toward the cool of dusk. He didn't think he'd dozed long; beside him, Abby and Angelique still slept. But every nerve vibrated with awareness. In the short time he'd lost his fight against sleep, something in the environment around them had changed.

All around them was silent—too silent. No birds sang. No lizards skittered on the rocks. No flies buzzed. The hair on the back of his neck rose, and he sat up straighter and started to turn around.

Hard metal pressed against the back of his head. "Don't move or I will blow your head off," a man said, in slightly accented English. "Give me the baby and I will think about letting you live."

Chapter Eleven

Abby gasped and clutched Angelique to her shoulder. The infant mewled and burrowed closer to her. An unfamiliar hand tightened on Abby's shoulder and she wrenched away and whirled to face an older Hispanic man. He held a gun to Michael's head. "Give the baby to me or I will kill your friend," he said. He held out his free hand for the baby.

"Who are you?" she demanded, clutching Angelique even more tightly to her. "What do you want with this baby?"

"You can call me El Jefe. Now give her to me or your friend will die."

"Don't give her to him." Michael spoke through gritted teeth. He still sat with his back to the man, his head wrenched to one side by the pressure of the gun barrel against his skull. But his eyes remained fixed on her, calm and determined.

Abby struggled to her feet and took a step back to put more distance between her and the man with the gun. She looked from him to Michael. Michael's face was pale, but nothing else about him betrayed agitation or fear. He'd gathered his legs under him, as if preparing to pounce. "Don't do it," he said again.

"Give her to me!" El Jefe insisted, and jabbed his weapon into Michael, who winced.

"What do you want with her?" Abby asked. She wrapped both arms around the baby. "She's an infant. She cries and wets her diaper. You don't look like a man who has time to change diapers."

"I will return her to her mother. She can take care of her."

Abby stared. Mariposa would certainly know how to take care of her own baby, but would this man really return the child to her? He was one of her jailers—the man who had ordered her to fetch water. Mariposa had wanted the child to be away from him.

"Her mother gave her to me to care for," Abby said. "I can't just hand her over to a stranger."

"You will give her to me!" He shoved the gun again, but this time Michael jerked his head to the side and swung his fist up and back, jamming it into the gunman's nose. El Jefe screamed, a wild, almost girlish sound, and blood poured from his broken nose. Michael shoved him back and grabbed for the weapon.

For an agonizingly long minute the two men struggled for the gun, rolling on the ground while Abby watched, heart in her throat, tensing herself for the explosion of the gun firing. She could have pulled her own weapon, but she didn't trust herself to get off a clear shot. El Jefe swore and struggled to grasp the weapon, but Michael was bigger and stronger, and he wasn't also fighting the pain and bleeding from a broken nose. At last, the older man gave up the fight, covering his face with his hands and shouting in Spanish.

Michael stood over him, breathing hard. "Who are you?" he demanded.

The man didn't look up, though he was no longer shouting, only muttering nonstop.

"Shut up and tell me who you are," Michael said.

The baby began to wail, and Abby rocked her in her arms, trying to comfort her. "Is she all right?" Michael asked.

"She's just hungry." And she was going to get a lot hungrier if they didn't get away from here soon.

Michael turned his attention back to the gunman, changing his line of questioning. "How did you get here?" he asked. "Where is your truck?"

Abby's spirits lifted. Of course. The man must have a vehicle somewhere nearby. A vehicle that could return them to safety—if they could find a road. But even the dirt tracks that crisscrossed the area must eventually lead somewhere. They could cover more ground searching in a vehicle than on foot.

"Why should I tell you anything?" the man asked.

"Answer my questions or I'll kill you." Michael's voice was hard; Abby shivered. She believed him.

"Kill me and you'll still be stuck out here with no way to leave," the man sneered. The bleeding had slowed. He patted gingerly at his nose, wincing.

A point for the bad guy. Abby looked around, hoping she'd spot the glint of sunlight off a truck hood or windshield, or maybe even see the vehicle, sitting in plain sight. Maybe it was too much to hope that the vehicle would come equipped with a GPS and a phone, but a woman could dream, couldn't she?

But instead of a lone truck sitting on the otherwise deserted plain, she saw something even better. "Michael, I think your friends finally found us," she said.

He kept the gun leveled on his prisoner, but glanced

over his shoulder at the line of Cruisers snaking across the desert. Then he pointed the weapon up and fired three shots. The baby wailed and Abby's own ears rang, but the signal had worked; the line of vehicles sped up, headed straight toward them.

"Now we'll deal— Stop!"

At Michael's shout, Abby turned. The gunman was running away, speeding over the rough ground like a jackrabbit, out of reach within seconds. Michael started across the rocks after him.

"Michael, no!" Abby said. "He's got too much of a head start. You can deal with him later."

"We may not have another chance." But he stopped and came to stand beside her. Together, they watched the Cruisers stop and park by the creek, then they walked down to meet them.

Graham greeted them as they picked their way across the creek. "What are you two doing out here?" he asked.

"Never mind that." Michael passed his boss, headed toward the trucks. "We need to try to catch up with the man who just ran away from here."

"What man?" Graham asked.

"He calls himself El Jefe. I'm pretty sure he's the guy who was in charge of this camp. If we can get him to talk, we may be able to break this case wide-open."

Graham and Michael left in Graham's Cruiser, leaving Abby with Carmen and Marco.

"Is that a baby?" Carmen stared at the bundle in Abby's arms.

"Her name is Angelique." Abby arranged the shawl to shade the infant's face. "And we really need to find some formula and feed her."

"Where did you get her?" Carmen smiled and stroked one of Angelique's tiny hands.

"Her mother was one of the workers camped here," Abby said. "How did you two ever find us?"

"We've been following the tracks of the trucks," Marco said. "We found Dance's Cruiser, wrecked and burning in a wash almost ten miles from here. We've been searching ever since."

"There was a camp of workers here," Abby said. "Four trailers—about two dozen people. Some men with trucks came and moved them this morning."

"Those must have been the trucks we were following." Marco joined them. "The tracks led right to here."

"Did the tracks lead from the destroyed Cruiser?" Abby asked.

"We found the tracks while we were trying to figure out how the Cruiser ended up in that wash," Marco said.

"But how did you two end up here without the Cruiser, and with a baby?" Carmen asked.

"It's a long story." Abby sighed. She was hot, tired, hungry and thirsty. "Right now, we need to get this child to a safe place."

She followed them to Marco's vehicle and climbed into the backseat. Angelique fussed and squirmed. "Somebody's not happy," Carmen said.

"She's hungry and her diaper needs changing," Abby said. "And she probably misses her mother." Mariposa probably missed her baby, too. Where was she now— and why had that man wanted her?

"Who's the guy Graham and Michael took off after?" Marco asked.

"He was in charge of the workers in the camp. He supervised the move. We hid and watched them hook up the trailers and drive off. I fell asleep and when I woke up, he was there, and had a gun on Michael. He demanded we give him the baby. When I refused, he threatened to kill Michael, but Michael broke his nose and took his gun. Your arrival distracted us enough he ran off."

When they reached the road and phone service, Carmen called headquarters. "Lance, I need you to run into town and buy a couple cans of baby formula, bottles and nipples, some baby wipes and a box of diapers." She looked over her shoulder at Angelique. "Size two." She grinned. "Yes, they're for a baby. Now, don't waste time arguing. We need these right away." She hung up the phone. "That's probably the oddest thing anyone's ever asked him to do. I wish I could see his face when he gets to the store and finds out how many different kinds of diapers there are. Let's hope he gets something that will work."

"You seem to know a lot about them," Marco said.

"I've got six younger brothers and sisters and half a dozen nieces and nephews," she said. "I've changed plenty of diapers in my day."

Abby cuddled the fussy baby closer. "We're going to make you more comfortable soon, little one," she said. She only hoped they'd be able to find Mariposa and reunite mother and child before it was too late.

MICHAEL STARED ACROSS the empty prairie. They hadn't found so much as a tire track that they could link to the man who had held him at gunpoint and tried to take the baby. "He couldn't have just vanished," he said.

"If he is the man in charge of the workers, he probably knows this country a lot better than we do," Graham said. He put his hand on Michael's shoulder. "Come on. Let's go back to headquarters."

"We need to go back to the campsite first. There's a bucket there that may have this guy's fingerprints on it. Maybe we'll come up with a match."

They returned to the camp and Michael retrieved the bucket from under the bush. "I'll get a team out to go over this place," Graham said.

"It's pretty clean, but maybe they'll find something," Michael said. He didn't like giving up the search for El Jefe so soon, but he doubted more time wandering around out here would bring them any closer to the man. He followed Graham back to the Cruiser.

"What happened to your face?" Graham asked.

Michael put a hand to the gash on his cheek. "I fell into a drainage. That's when I lost the phone and radio."

"Was that before or after you acquired the baby?"

"After."

"Where did the baby come from?"

"One of the workers gave it to Abby, when the bosses showed up to move them. Then we were spotted and had to make a run for it."

"But the guy in charge caught up with you?"

Michael shook his head. "That was later. Without the GPS or a phone or maps, we were lost. We needed water, so staying near the creek made sense. I knew you'd send someone to look for us when I didn't report in this evening. In the meantime, I figured the boss man might come back to look for us. I knew he'd stolen my truck, so he probably guessed we couldn't go far. I planned to get the jump on him when he returned, but it didn't work out that way." He fought down anger at himself for making such a hash of the whole day. Had his attraction to Abby distracted him so much he'd been less diligent?

"We'll find him," Graham said. "What did he want with the baby?"

"No idea. He said he would return her to her mother, but Abby got the impression the mom thought the baby would be safer with her."

"The two of you can fill us in on the details when we get back to headquarters."

At ranger headquarters, they found Carmen feeding the baby a bottle while Abby, dressed in a black task-force polo and hiking shorts she must have borrowed from Carmen, ate a deli sandwich from a tray in the middle of the conference table. She set aside the sandwich when he walked in. "Did you find him?" she asked.

Michael shook his head and sagged into the chair across from her. He glanced toward the baby. "How's Angelique?"

"She is living up to her name and being a little angel," Carmen said. She positioned the baby over her shoulder and patted her back.

"She's happier now that's she's eaten and had a fresh diaper," Abby said. "Though I don't think you're going to want your bandanna back."

"I have more where that came from." He helped himself to a sandwich. Abby's leaves and roots hadn't tasted as bad as he'd feared, but they hadn't been very filling.

Graham pulled out the chair at the head of the table. "Tell me about this man," he said.

"I'm pretty sure he's the one who was ordering everyone else around," Michael said. "I didn't have binoculars, but he was tall and thin, and was the only one wearing a white shirt."

"And he didn't say why he wanted the baby?"

"He said he would return her to her mother," Abby said.

"Maybe he's the father," Carmen said. When the others stared at her, she shrugged. "Even criminals can love their children. Or maybe he loves the mother and she changed her mind about giving up her child, and she sent him to retrieve the baby."

"Or maybe he sees the child as a tie to him and his operation and he wants to get rid of her," Marco said.

Abby shuddered at the idea. "What harm is an infant going to do?" she asked. "She can't testify against him."

"She might share his DNA, and that might tie him to a crime we don't even know about yet," Marco said.

Abby tried to push away the thought that the man might have wanted to harm Angelique. But a man who made slaves of other people might not balk at killing a baby.

"You said you were following tracks," Michael said. "Where did they lead?"

"Nowhere," Marco said. "Once they reached the highway, we lost them."

"But now that we know what we're looking for, it won't be so easy to hide that many people and trailers," Michael said.

"Unless they dismantled everything and took everyone straight to Denver or another big city," Carmen said. "Your guy could be long gone."

Michael shook his head. "I don't think so. He wanted Angelique badly enough to come back by himself to retrieve her."

"That part doesn't make sense to me," Marco said. "He had to have others helping him when he moved the camp."

"He had at least five other men with guns," Michael said.

"Then why didn't he bring them with him to retrieve the baby?" Marco asked. "Even one other man with him would have increased his chances of success."

"Maybe he didn't want anyone to know about the baby," Abby said.

"But they already knew about the baby," Michael said. "Mariposa didn't try to hide her from the others, that I could tell."

Abby stood and went to take the sleeping infant from Carmen. Angelique hardly stirred as Abby cradled her close. "Maybe Carmen is right and he came back for Angelique because she's his child," she said. "If that's true, he might not want the others to know, or to suspect he had a soft spot for the baby."

"We don't know that," Michael said. "He might have intended to kill her."

"Then maybe he didn't want the others to know that, either." The idea made her sick to her stomach, but they would gain nothing by refusing to consider all possibilities.

"Whatever the reason he wanted her, it doesn't really matter," Carmen said.

"Why not?" Michael asked.

"Because we know the baby represents a weakness or a secret he doesn't want anyone else finding out about," Graham said. "If you know a man's weakness or secret, you can find a way to exploit it."

"But if he's already on his way to Denver…" Abby sent a questioning look to Graham.

"I think Michael's hunch is right and he won't want to leave without the baby," Graham said. "We can use that against him."

Abby smiled down at the child, who had fallen back asleep. She'd never seen a more beautiful baby, with such long, dark lashes, and a perfect Cupid's bow of a mouth.

Aware that the room had fallen silent, she looked up to find everyone else looking at her—or rather, they were focused on the baby. "What is it?" she asked. "What's wrong?"

Graham cleared his throat. "If we spread the word around that you're keeping the baby for a while, and make you seem vulnerable, we could lure our guy out to take another chance. Only this time, we'd be waiting to capture him."

"You mean, use Angelique as bait to catch him?" She stared, sure she couldn't have heard them correctly.

Graham nodded. "You and Angelique, yes. Bait to catch what could be a very big fish."

Chapter Twelve

"No!" Abby and Michael spoke at the same time.

"It's too dangerous." Michael shoved back his chair and stood. "She could be hurt."

"He's right. You can't take that kind of risk with a baby," Abby said.

"I wasn't talking about Angelique." Michael moved around the table to stand beside her. "It's too dangerous for you *and* the baby." His eyes met hers and she knew he was speaking not as a law enforcement officer, but as a man who cared for her. The realization moved her, but she looked away. This wasn't a time to let sentiment cloud her judgment.

"We'd have someone from the team with you 24/7," Graham said. "And other team members stationed nearby. If our man makes a move, we'd be on him."

"It's our best chance to catch this guy," Marco said. "If we get to him, we're that much closer to finding the person in charge of the operation. We can stop him from enslaving other workers."

"Can you help Mariposa and the others?" she asked.

"There's a good chance we can," Graham said.

Abby looked down at the sleeping infant. As much as she cared for the child, she wasn't in a position to take her permanently. The baby needed to be with her mother, as long as her mother could take care of her.

Michael's hand rested heavy on her shoulder. "Abby, don't do it," he said. "Don't risk it. We'll find some other way."

"I can't risk anything happening to Angelique," she said. "We don't know what this man's intentions are toward her."

"She's right." Carmen spoke up. "We'll need to use a decoy for the baby and move Angelique into temporary foster care."

"Agreed," Graham said. "I don't want the child to come to harm. And I don't want you harmed, either, Abby. I promise we'll protect you. But the final decision is yours."

Michael's hand on her shoulder tightened, but he remained silent. That silence—his faith in her ability to make the right decision—moved her more than any words could have. "I'll do it," she said. "As long as Angelique is somewhere safe."

"Abby…" Michael spoke so softly she might have been the only one who heard.

She turned to face him. "I want to stop these people," she said. "I want Mariposa and Angelique to have a better life. If I can do something to help them, then I have to act."

"I want that, too," he said. "But I want you to stay safe."

"I'll be safe," she said. "I know you've got my back." She deliberately repeated the words he'd told her earlier.

"Carmen, you take care of transferring Angelique to foster care," Graham said. "We'll have to manage the switch without anyone who might be watching realizing what's going on."

"They make some pretty realistic-looking baby dolls," Carmen said. "I'll get one of those and a layette. Abby will pretend to care for it as she would Angelique."

"I might as well go back to my trailer in the park campground," Abby said. "That will make it easier for this guy to get to me, and put me closer to all of you."

"I'll go with you," Michael said.

Graham gave him a hard look. "It might be better to send someone else."

"No, sir. I can do this."

Graham's expression remained grim, but he nodded. "All right. Go on to the trailer. Carmen and Marco will meet you there later to pick up the baby and substitute the doll. Randall, you and Lance can take turns watching Abby's trailer. I doubt this guy will try anything so soon, but stay on your guard."

"Yes, sir."

Abby carried Angelique, while Michael gathered up the diapers, formula and other baby supplies, along with an overnight bag from his locker. "I'll be sure to bring a car seat when we come to get her," Carmen said, following them to her Cruiser, which Michael was borrowing until his could be replaced. "Right now, you don't have far to go to the campground."

Everything at her trailer looked just as she'd left it, though Michael insisted on searching all around the outside and checking out the inside while she waited with the baby. "I don't think anyone's been here since you left," he said at last, and held the door open for her to enter.

The baby started crying before they were through the door. "I think it's time for a diaper change," Abby said.

"I'll get the stuff out of the car."

When he returned, she was still standing in the middle of the room with the wailing baby. "What's wrong?" he asked.

"I don't know where to put her. I'm not exactly set up for a baby."

Michael looked around at the compact space, then set the box of supplies on the table and began emptying it out. "We can put her in here. It's about the size of a bassinet, and she won't fall out."

"You're brilliant." She grinned at him.

"I have my moments." He grabbed a towel from the counter and used it to line the box, then slid it toward her. "Instant cradle."

"Hand me a diaper first."

While she changed the baby, he put away the formula and other supplies. She wedged the box between the dinette and sofa and settled the baby inside. Michael sat beside her on the sofa. "Now what?" he asked.

"Why don't you take a shower, then I'll grab one," she said.

"Are you suggesting I need one?" He pretended to look offended.

"No comment." She stood. "I'm going to make some tea. The bathroom is kind of small, but I think you'll find everything you need."

While she filled the teakettle and took a mug from the cabinet, she listened to the water beating against the wall of the shower and tried not to think of Michael, naked, just on the other side of that barrier. But once the image was fixed in her mind, of his sculpted shoulders and arms and muscular abs, she could think of nothing else. Her imagination filled in the rest of the picture, until desire settled over her in a languid heat.

She forced her mind away from the fantasy and savored the memory of the kiss they'd shared earlier in the day. In that moment, kissing him had seemed the most natural thing in the world—the thing she had wanted most. She'd lusted after men before, but she couldn't remember ever feeling so close to one. She hadn't been in a serious relationship in years—before she went to war. A lifetime ago, when she was a different person.

Was it only because circumstance and danger had thrown them together that she felt this way? Did she feel so comfortable with him because they were both veterans? Or because he'd saved her life when she was injured in Afghanistan? Was he right, and fate had somehow brought them together? She slipped her hand into her pocket and caressed the little rabbit figure. All these years, she'd held on to the token, feeling it was somehow important. Had the caring the gift of the rabbit represented now grown into something more—even into love?

The bathroom door opened and he emerged wearing only a pair of low-slung jeans, toweling his hair. She stared at the drops of water glinting in the dusting of brown hair across his muscular chest and her mouth went dry. Michael Dance in uniform was an impressive sight, but Michael Dance half naked was enough to make her forget her own name.

He tossed the towel aside and grinned, and she blushed, sure he had caught her staring. "I feel almost human again," he said. He moved toward her at the same time she tried to leave the kitchen area, and they collided. The trailer suddenly felt too small to contain them. She mumbled an apology and tried to slip past, and he put out a hand to steady her, freezing her in place.

He smoothed his hand down her arm and a tremor rocked her. Her skin burned where he touched her, and she fought the urge to lean into him, to lose herself in the feel of his body against hers. She looked up and realized he'd shaved, the scent of his shaving cream filling her senses.

"Tight fit," he said.

Why did her traitorous mind turn those words into a come-on, with thoughts of how well the two of them would fit together? She looked away—at the floor, the wall—anything but those sensuous lips, beckoning. If she started to kiss him now, she'd forget all about the shower, and the baby, and everything but slaking the desire that rocked through her.

"I'll just, um, take my shower now," she said, pushing past him.

"Don't you need to wait for the water to warm up again?"

"That's okay." A little cold water might be just what she needed.

The water was warm enough, though. She took her time in the shower, washing her hair and shaving her legs. *As if I was prepping for a big date*, she thought.

But this was no casual date. Michael was spending the night here in her trailer. Considering the electricity they'd managed to generate with only a brief touch, she wasn't foolish enough to believe they wouldn't act on that attraction at some point. But when—and what might happen afterward—was anyone's guess.

She slipped into yoga pants and a T-shirt and blow-dried her hair, but didn't bother with makeup. She didn't want to seem obvious or desperate. Besides, the man had seen her at her absolute worst. A little mascara and lipstick weren't going to change his opinion of her.

She opened the bathroom door and was surprised to hear humming. She froze, listening, and made out a few words. "Hush, little baby, don't say a word. Papa's gonna buy you a mockingbird."

She peeked around the door and stared at Michael, standing by the sofa, holding the baby. The infant looked impossibly small in his arms, smiling up at him and cooing as he sang softly. More priceless still was the look on his face, the stern lines and angular features softened in a smile of such tenderness it brought a lump to her throat.

He turned and saw her standing there, and the tips of his ears turned pink. "She was fussy," he said by way of explanation.

"Obviously, you've made a conquest." She joined him in front of the sofa and he tried to hand the baby over, but she waved him off. "Oh, no, she looks very happy where she is."

She sat, and he sat beside her. Angelique gurgled happily. "I've never spent much time around babies," he said.

"Then, you're a natural," she said. "You'll make a good father one day."

He was silent for a moment, both of them watching the baby, who stared back with her solemn brown eyes. "Do you think about it much—having kids, raising a family?" he asked.

"Sometimes," she admitted. "More lately, now that

my life is beginning to settle down. Before, when I was in the army, and later, after I was injured, even the possibility of that kind of stability seemed so far away."

"Yeah, I haven't exactly had the kind of life that makes a wife and kids seem like a good idea."

"I have to finish graduate school and find a job— figure out what I'm going to do with the rest of my life." She leaned over and stroked the infant's satin-soft cheek. "But sometimes I wonder if those things are just excuses to keep me from focusing on all the emotional, personal things that are harder to deal with."

"I know what you mean," he said. "I can deal with the toughest situations in my job, but when it comes to relationships...sometimes that's a lot scarier."

Their eyes met, and her heart sped up, fluttering in her chest. "Do I scare you?" she asked, keeping her tone light, a little flirtatious.

"Oh, yeah." He cupped her cheek in his hand. "But I'm a big believer in the importance of facing your fears."

He lowered his head toward her, but the sound of tires on gravel made him straighten, instantly alert. "Someone's coming," he said, and handed her the baby.

He stood and walked to the window and peered out the blinds. Abby clutched the baby to her, aware that the vehicle had stopped outside her door.

"Hey, it's just us," a woman called. "We came by to see how you're settling in with the baby."

At the sound of Carmen's familiar voice, Michael's shoulders relaxed. He pulled on a T-shirt, then went to the door.

Carmen came in, followed by Lance. He carried a large cardboard box labeled Diapers.

"We brought you some more diapers and formula," he said, his voice loud in the evening silence.

He set the box on the table, made sure all the blinds were drawn, then took the top off the diaper box to reveal a realistic-looking baby doll, wrapped in a blanket identical to the one that swaddled Angelique. "It's a doll called My Real Baby," Carmen said. "Isn't it a kick?"

She lifted the doll out of the box, handling it as if it were a real baby, and passed it to Abby. "From a distance, I'm sure no one could tell the difference," she said.

Abby cradled the doll and turned to look at Angelique, who rested in the box on the sofa. "I'm going to miss the real baby, though," she said. "Where are you taking her?"

"The state put me in touch with a woman in Grand Junction who specializes in temporary foster care for infants," Carmen said. "She'll be safe there."

Safer than she would be here with her and Michael, Abby knew, but still, she hated to see her leave.

Carmen picked up Angelique and cooed at her, then transferred her to the diaper box. "I don't guess you've heard anything from our friend?" she said as she tucked blankets around the baby.

"Nothing," Michael said. "But we don't even know if he knows she's here yet."

"We talked it up in town," Lance said. "I stopped for gas and told everyone there about the baby we'd found."

"You'd think he lived for gossip." Carmen elbowed the younger agent in the side. "Everyone was all ears. Maybe some of the talk will get back to our guy."

"Maybe so."

"Call if you need anything." Lance fit the lid back on the diaper box and picked it up.

"Take good care of her." Abby curled her hands into fists to keep from reaching for the baby.

"We will," Carmen said. "See you tomorrow."

They left, and Michael shut and locked the door behind them. Abby sank onto the sofa and listened to the sound of their tires gradually fade to silence. She blinked hard, fighting tears, but they spilled over and rolled down her cheeks.

"Hey, what's wrong?" Michael hurried to her side.

"I didn't even get to say goodbye." She choked back a sob. He took her hand and patted it, but as she continued to sob harder, he pulled her to him. She buried her face against his chest. "I know it's stupid," she said. "I hardly know her, but I felt responsible for her."

"Shh. It's okay." He smoothed his hand down her hair and rocked her against him. "Of course you miss her. It's hard not knowing what's going to happen to her."

She raised her head to look at him. "You understand."

"I try." He kissed her cheek, but she turned and found his lips. She kissed him greedily, hungrily, wanting to blot out the sadness, to forget for a little while about the baby and Mariposa and a stranger who might want her dead.

He responded with the same fervor, wrapping his arms around her and pulling her tight against his chest. The tip of his tongue traced the seam of her lips and she opened to him, tasting the butterscotch candy he liked. They kissed until she was trembling and light-headed, her body humming with awareness of him, but still she wanted more.

She slid her hand beneath his T-shirt and pressed her

palm against his stomach, feeling the crisp line of hair that disappeared beneath the waistband of his jeans. He kissed his way to her ear and said, his voice low and husky with need, "If you keep that up, I'm not going to be able to stop."

"I don't want to stop," she said. "I want to make love to you." As if to prove her words, she pushed him back against the sofa, her body slanted over his. He dragged one hand up, over her rib cage, and cupped her breast through her thin T-shirt, the tip a hard bead pressed against his palm. He flicked his thumb back and forth across it, sending little shock waves of desire rocketing through her. Her breath came in gasps, and her eyes drifted shut as she surrendered to the onslaught of sensation.

Then his mouth was on her, the combination of heat and moisture and the gentle abrasion of the fabric driving her wild. She let out a soft moan and fumbled to remove the shirt. He sat up and helped her, then shed his own shirt, so they were both naked from the waist up.

"You're so beautiful." He slid his hands down her sides, as if cradling something precious. "So beautiful."

She believed he would have said the same thing if her body had been scarred like her face. The words wouldn't have been a lie; she believed when Michael looked at her, he saw more than what was on the surface. He always had; maybe that was why she'd fallen in love with him.

She stood and held out her hand. "Let's move to the bed, where we'll be more comfortable."

He grasped her hand and let her pull him up and lead him to the bed at the other end of the trailer. She pulled back the covers and he started to follow, then hesitated. "What is it?" she asked.

"Just a second." He turned and slipped into the bathroom.

She took off her jeans and underwear, so that by the time he returned, she was sitting up in bed, naked.

His gaze took her in, and the wanting in his eyes made her tremble all over again. "What took you so long?" she said.

He held up a condom in a foil packet. "I had to get this from my overnight bag."

She smiled. "You think of everything."

"I was a Boy Scout, remember? Their motto is Be Prepared."

"Something tells me they weren't thinking of situations like this." She moved over to make room for him.

He stopped to shed his own jeans and her heart beat faster as she stared—while trying to appear not to stare—at his body. He was as gorgeous as her fantasies.

They lay on their sides facing each other, the dimmed reading lights on either side of the bed providing soft illumination. He traced his hand down the curve of her side, then cupped her bottom and drew her close once more. "I feel as if I've been waiting for this moment for a long time," he said. "Does that seem crazy?"

"No." She felt the same way. As if her reluctance to go out with other men had been because she hadn't met *him* yet. Maybe those frantic moments on a helicopter over Afghanistan had forged a bond too deep for understanding. She only knew that with him, she lost the shyness and desire to close herself off and hide away. She wanted to open to him, to reveal everything, to be with him, in this moment, as she'd never allowed her-self to be before.

"Make love to me," she whispered, and kissed him lightly on the lips.

He deepened the kiss, and soon they were entwined, arms and legs wrapped around each other, hands and lips stroking, exploring. He pulled away only long enough to roll on the condom, then he drew her close once more and entered her. She wrapped her legs around him, wanting to shout in joy or triumph, but then he began to move and she lost all power of speech or thought. There was only wave after wave of wonder-ful sensation building within her.

Her climax was the largest wave, washing over her, filling her with light and life, then releasing her, float-ing. Soaring. He tightened his hold on her and found his own release, crying out her name. "Abby!"

Afterward, they remained entwined, her head pil-lowed on his arms, her fingers stroking his chest. "I wasn't sure I'd ever feel that wonderful again," she said.

"I'm glad you don't feel you have to hide anything from me." He traced the scar on her face with the tip of one finger. With a start, she realized she lay with that side of her face to the light, her hair tucked back behind her ear. Even in sleep, she usually lay so the scar was hidden. But though this position felt a little awkward—exposed—it didn't feel wrong.

She snuggled closer to him. "You've seen me at my worst and didn't run away," she said. "I guess I really don't have anything to hide."

"I'll always be here for you," he said. "I won't let anyone hurt you again."

MICHAEL WOKE EARLY, long habit preventing him from sleeping much past sunrise. Gray light filled the trailer, and outside a bird was singing a morning chorus. Abby lay curled on her side beside him, her back to him, her face half buried in the covers. He rolled over, trying not to disturb her, and studied her sleeping form. Maybe he should pinch himself to make sure he wasn't dreaming. He'd had similar dreams often enough over the years. Sometimes he'd worried something was wrong with him; who let the memory of one woman with whom he'd never even spoken possess him so?

But it didn't matter why his attraction to Abby had stuck with him all these years, only that she was here with him now. Whether fate or chance had brought them together, he'd be her guardian and her lover. Neither of them would be alone again.

She stirred, as if feeling his gaze on her, and rolled onto her back and smiled up at him. "How long have you been watching me?" she asked.

"Only a few minutes." He moved closer; her skin was warm from sleep, so soft and smooth.

"Mmm. You're definitely awake." Smiling, she reached down to stroke him.

He resisted the urge to pull her onto him right away, and kissed her shoulder. "You're definitely nicer to wake up to than my alarm."

"Give me a second. I'll be right back." She patted his shoulder and slid out of bed. He rolled onto his back and stared up at the ceiling of the trailer, which was only a few feet above his head. He didn't want thoughts of the world outside to intrude on this moment, but of course they did. He wondered how Angelique was doing, and if El Jefe thought she was still with Abby.

She slipped back into bed, smelling of mint tooth-paste, her hair combed and the sleep washed from her eyes. "My turn," he said, and hurried to banish his own morning breath and retrieve another condom from his bag.

When he returned to the bed, she waited with open arms. He pulled her close, savoring the sensation of her breasts pillowed against his chest, the nipples already erect and hard. She draped her thigh over his, press-ing close, eager. "What time do you have to report in?" she asked.

"Not for another hour or so," he said. "We have plenty of time."

"Time for what?" she teased.

He snugged her more tightly against him. "Time for me to show you more of what you've been missing."

"Or maybe I'll be the one to show you a thing or two." She untangled herself from him and sat up, then pushed him back against the pillows and straddled him.

"Oh, you think so." He caressed her waist.

"I wasn't a biology major for nothing. Hand me that condom," she said. "Class is in session."

THEY FELL ASLEEP again and woke to the buzzing of Mi-chael's phone as it vibrated against the bedside table. He rolled over and snatched it up while Abby propped herself on her elbow and watched. She felt warm and relaxed and a little sore, but in a good way. She smiled, remembering how the soreness had come about. Clearly, all she needed was a little more practice with Michael to be in excellent shape.

"Nothing going on here," he said. "Did you get Angelique placed all right?…I'll tell Abby.…She slept fine, as far as I know.…Now, how would I know that?" The tips of his ears flushed red and Abby covered her mouth, smothering a giggle. She loved that he could still get flustered like that.

He hung up the phone and rolled onto his back. "That was Carmen. She said Angelique was settling in well when she left her last night. The woman is in her forties and has two teenagers. Angelique will be the only baby with her right now and seemed to really take to the woman."

"Thanks for letting me know. What did she say that made you blush?"

He turned even redder. "She wanted to know if I kept you up late last night—and if your bed was comfortable."

"So she knew you were attracted to me?"

"I think the whole team knew. I'm not so good at hiding my feelings."

"I guess I was the one who was slow on the uptake," she said. "At least for a while." She sat up. "And though I'd like to stay in bed with you all day, I guess we'd better get up. What's the plan for the day?"

"I guess you should be seen out and about with the baby. We want to give El Jefe every chance to find you and make his move."

"It won't be the same as having a real baby to hold, but I'll do my best."

Fifteen minutes later, they were both dressed and Abby had coffee brewing. "I'm going to go outside and look around," Michael said. He slid his gun into the holster on his utility belt. "I never heard anything last night, but you never know."

"We were both a little preoccupied last night," she said.

"True."

He opened the door and stepped out into the clear, thin light of early morning. The air still held a touch of the night's chill, and smelled of piñon and cedar. The campsites on either side of Abby's trailer were empty, and trees screened the view from any other site. Her car sat parked beside the picnic table and the empty fire ring, the borrowed Cruiser next to it. Nothing looked out of place.

He turned to survey the trailer and his heartbeat sped up. A folded sheet of paper fluttered against the door, held in place by a piece of blue tape.

He returned to the trailer and retrieved a knife from the drawer in the kitchen. "What is it?" Abby asked. She followed him to the door. "Is something wrong?"

"Someone left you a note." He slid the blade of the knife beneath the tape, detaching the note from the door. Holding it by the corner, he unfolded it and scanned the brief message.

"What does it say?" Abby stood on tiptoe, trying to see over his shoulder. "Let me see."

He held the note out to her. "Don't touch it. Just read it."

She frowned. "I can't. It's in Spanish."

He'd forgotten for a moment she didn't read the language. "It's from Mariposa. She wants you to meet her. She says she's safe and can take the baby now."

Chapter Thirteen

Abby stared at the note, wishing she could read the words for herself. "Does this mean she managed to get away from the people who were holding her prisoner?" she asked. "How did she know where to find me?"

"She didn't." Michael tapped the note with his index finger. "This is a fake. A trick to lure you away to a place where it will be easier to kidnap Angelique and get rid of you."

Her initial excitement over the note faded. Of course he was right. "Mariposa couldn't have known I was here," she said.

"Of course not. If she did, why not knock on the door and ask to see her baby right away?"

"I can understand why she wouldn't do that," Abby said. "If she's in the United States illegally, she wouldn't want to risk running into someone who works for border patrol. I mean, your car is parked out front."

"Point taken. But I don't believe she wrote this note," he said.

"Or she wrote it because someone forced her to," Abby said. Had El Jefe convinced Mariposa it was safe for her to have her child with her again? "I wish I knew why that man wants the baby."

"Does it matter?" Michael asked. "Even if it's because he's the father and loves her, what kind of life could she have with her mother as a prisoner?"

Abby hugged her arms across her chest, suddenly cold despite the growing warmth from the sun. "What do we do now?" she asked.

"I want to show this note to Graham and the rest of the team," he said. "Let's bundle up the baby and go over to headquarters."

Abby went through the motions of arranging the doll in the sling around her body. "This feels weird," she said.

"It may feel weird, but it looks real," he said. "That's all that counts. Just keep up the charade while we're outside, in case anyone is watching."

So she cradled the doll to her and pretended to coo and fuss over it as she walked to the Cruiser and climbed into the passenger seat. Michael started the engine. "Do you really think someone is watching us?" she asked.

"That note tells me they are." He checked the mirrors, then backed out of his parking spot.

"Then, they know you spent the night in my trailer."

He glanced at her. "Does that bother you? That other people know we were together?"

"No. But won't they be suspicious? The Cruiser makes it obvious you're with the task force, even if they didn't recognize you before."

"Just because I'm with the task force doesn't mean I was on duty last night. We're allowed to have personal lives. But just in case whoever is spying on us has doubts..." He shifted the Cruiser into Park and leaned across the seat and kissed her.

She let out a small gasp of surprise, then relaxed into him, reaching up one hand to twine her fingers in his hair as he deepened the kiss, his lips firm against her own, tantalizing and once again awakening desire she'd thought long dormant. When at last he broke contact, she stared up at him, a little breathless. "I'd say that was pretty convincing."

"I wasn't acting, if you were worried about that," he said.

"No." He hadn't been acting last night, either. The connection between them had been very real—and a little unnerving, if she was being completely honest with herself. She wasn't sure she was ready to jump into a relationship, especially with a man whose life was so complicated. She'd gotten through the years since her return from the war by keeping her life simple—no ties, no long-term commitments, no lasting obligations to anyone but herself. It was a shallow way to live, but a safe one. Michael was luring her into something much deeper—and scarier.

At ranger headquarters, they found Simon hunched over a computer in the front room. He frowned at the doll Abby unwrapped from the sling. "What are you two up to?" he asked.

"Someone left a suspicious note on Abby's door last night," Michael said. "Where's the G man?"

"I'm here." Graham emerged from his office. He looked tired, as if he hadn't slept well. Was he worried about her or Angelique? Abby wondered. Or did some new development in the case trouble him?

"This was taped to the door of Abby's trailer this morning." Michael handed Graham the note.

The captain took a pair of reading glasses from his

front pocket and slipped them on, then studied the torn scrap of paper. "Do you know who left it?" He looked at Abby. "Did you hear anyone? See anyone?"

"No, sir," Michael answered, brisk and military.

"No," Abby echoed, and looked away, focused on rearranging the blankets around the baby doll, as if doing so was an urgent task she could put off no longer. She marveled at Michael's ability to keep his expression neutral, revealing nothing. For much of the time last night, the two of them had been so focused on each other there could have been a drag race on the road outside her campsite and she wouldn't have noticed.

"Weren't Lance and Randall watching the place all night?" Michael asked.

"They were," Graham said. "If they'd seen anything suspicious, they would have called it in." He laid the note on the table. "We'll dust this for prints, though I doubt we'll come up with anything."

"We got a match off that bucket that was left behind at the camp," Simon said.

"Who is it?" Michael asked.

"The woman's prints didn't pull up anything, but the man's belong to Raul Meredes." Simon turned to Michael. "Ever hear of him?"

Michael shook his head. "No. Who is he?"

"He has ties to the Milenio cartel out of Guadalajara," Graham said. "He was the chief suspect in the murder of a sheriff's deputy on the Texas border, but they couldn't make the charges stick."

"He's been operating on both sides of the border for years," Simon said. "Smuggling drugs and people."

"I don't think he wrote this note." Carmen leaned

over Graham's shoulder and read the note. "The writing looks feminine to me."

"It does to me, too," Abby said. "But El Jefe—Meredes—could have forced her to write it. Or another woman might have written it."

"I don't suppose you saw any sign of a blonde American woman in the group at those trailers," Graham said.

"You mean Lauren Starling?" Michael asked. "So she's still missing."

"The Denver police are reluctant to call it a missing person. Apparently, she has a history of erratic behavior, and she pulled a disappearing act like this before. But the family is starting to make noise, so they've asked us to take a closer look—not that we have anything to go on. The car is clean—no note, map or anything indicating her intentions."

"I don't think she was at the camp," Abby said. "Everyone I saw had dark hair and looked Latino."

"Just thought I'd ask." Graham turned his attention back to the note. "What do we do about this?"

"It's a fake," Michael said. "Someone is trying to lure Abby and the baby into danger."

"The baby is safe," Carmen said. "Whatever we decide to do won't endanger her."

"We aren't going to do anything," Michael said. "It's too dangerous."

Abby froze in the act of tucking a blanket more securely around the doll. The voice was Michael's, but it could have been her father, telling her she couldn't join the army, or men in her unit protesting that she wasn't capable of leading a patrol, family members saying she couldn't go away to college, or she shouldn't study biology, or do research in remote areas. All her life, people had been telling her what she couldn't do or what she wasn't capable of. *Female* or *beautiful* or *wounded* had been labels they used against her that only made her want to dig in her heels and prove them wrong.

"We've had another new development, which may or may not be related," Graham said.

Abby stopped fussing with the blanket and turned to face the captain once more. He hadn't agreed with Michael. In fact, he'd changed the subject.

"What new development?" Michael arched one eyebrow and waited.

"Richard Prentice has blocked a park service road that crosses his land," Graham said. "It's a public road that predates the park. It's the shortest route—the only route, really—to some rare petroglyphs in the canyon. A group from the University of Denver has been studying them off and on for the past two years. This morning, they found barricades blocking the road. Prentice's lawyers filed an injunction yesterday and a judge ordered the road closed, pending a hearing."

"Why is he closing the road now, after all this time?" Michael asked.

"Because he can," Simon said.

"Or because he's doing something he doesn't want anyone getting close enough to see," Lance said.

"Something like what?" Abby asked.

Graham frowned. Maybe he was weighing the wisdom of discussing a task force case with a civilian. Abby wished she'd kept her mouth shut. Now he might send her from the room. "Abby is part of this now," Carmen said. "And she knows how to keep what we say confidential."

"Of course," she agreed, and sent Carmen a grateful look.

Graham nodded. "Sensors we planted on the public road to measure traffic into the park indicate an increase in the number of vehicles turning onto Prentice's ranch," he said. "More than we can credit to a few college students on their way to the petroglyphs, or Prentice and his various workers and visitors."

"Who do you think is going in and out of there?" Michael asked.

"We've been doing frequent drive-bys, but we haven't seen much," Randall said.

"Prentice complains loudly and long—to the press, to government officials and to anyone else who will listen—that we're harassing him," Simon said.

"We've tried taking a look from the air, but we haven't spotted anything suspicious—yet," Graham said.

"Do you think whatever is going on there has anything to do with Mariposa and Raul Meredes and the illegal workers we saw in the trailers?" Abby asked.

"We just don't know," Graham said.

"But those trailers and people had to go somewhere when they left that wash," Simon said. "Prentice's ranch makes a convenient place for them to disappear quickly. We can't find anyone who saw them after they left you two that morning, and once they hit the park road, the tracks disappeared."

"If I go to this meeting with Mariposa or Meredes or whoever, you can find out more," Abby said. "You might learn something really useful that would help crack the case."

"No!" Michael's protest drowned out whatever

Graham had been about to say. Even a stern look from his boss didn't make him back down. "We shouldn't endanger a civilian," he added.

"This is what we wanted all along, isn't it?" Abby asked. "To lure him into the open so that you can capture him."

"It's too risky," Michael said. "Our original plan was to lure him here, where we have more control over everything. If you move into his territory, the control shifts to him."

Was he so worried about control over the outcome of this plan—or control over her? She tried to tell herself Michael wasn't like that, but her past experiences with the men in her life told her otherwise. After all, how well did she really know this man? He'd first made a claim on her because he'd saved her life. In the golden afterglow of lovemaking, had she misinterpreted an unhealthy obsession for love?

She forced herself to look directly at him, to try to read the true emotion in his dark eyes. But she found only stubbornness. "I'm not helpless," she said. "I've been in dangerous situations before. Much more dangerous. I'm trained to look after myself."

"You don't have an army behind you this time," he said. "Don't confuse foolishness with bravery."

The words stung like a slap. "You don't have a right to tell me what to do!" she protested.

"Abby's right." Graham stepped between them. "This could be the break we've been looking for. If we can get to Meredes, he could lead us to the person behind this whole operation."

"We might find a link between him and Prentice," Simon said.

"This might help save Mariposa and a lot of other innocent people," Abby said. "How could I not do it?"

"We'll set up the meeting for a neutral place," Graham said. "And we'll have plenty of our people watching, on guard if Meredes tries to pull anything."

"If you try to take him there, he's liable to use Abby as a hostage," Michael said.

"If we can't get to him without endangering her, we'll follow him after he leaves," Graham said.

"I want to do this," Abby said. "I want to help these people."

"I still don't think—"

But she didn't get to hear what he did or didn't think. Graham's phone rang, the old-fashioned clanging silencing them all. "Captain Ellison," he answered. He stood up straighter, shoulders tensed, expression alert. "Where?…How many?…We'll be right there."

He ended the call. "That was Randall. He and Marco think they've found the trailers from the camp, or at least some of them."

"Where?" Simon was the first to speak.

"Are there any people in them?" Carmen asked.

Graham turned to the map on the wall behind him. He studied it for a moment, then pointed to a spot on the edge of the parkland. "There's a wash through here. The trailers are there."

Michael joined Graham in front of the map. "That's on the very edge of Richard Prentice's ranch," he said, pointing to the white area marked Private Property on the map.

"And they almost certainly crossed Prentice's land on that road he closed in order to get there," Simon said.

"How did Randall and Marco get there?" Carmen asked.

"They hitched a ride on a BLM chopper," Graham said. "Someone who owed Randall a favor."

"The bigger question is, how are we going to get there?" Michael asked. "Prentice still has the road closed."

"Then we'll have to persuade him to open it." Graham fished car keys from his pocket. "Let's go. Michael, you'd better stay here with Abby."

"I'll come with you," Abby said.

"I can't let you do that," Graham said.

"You need Michael with you, and you can't leave me here unguarded as long as Meredes is looking for me and the baby. Instead of sacrificing one man to babysit me, let me come along. I promise to stay in the vehicle, out of your way." She hesitated, then added, "Please. I need to know if Mariposa is there—if she's safe."

Graham glanced at Michael, then back to Abby. "You can come, but you're to stay well away from the action. Ride with Simon."

"Thank you," she said.

"She can ride with me," Michael said.

"No. I need you focused on the job, not her," Graham said. "Carmen will ride with you. Now let's get going."

Abby tried to arrange the baby doll more comfortably in the sling as the others gathered their gear and prepared to head out. Michael approached her. "I just want to talk to you for a minute," he said in response to her wary look. He pulled her to a corner of the room, away from the others.

"I know what I'm getting into," she said. "I don't need you to protect me."

"I'm not saying you're not smart and capable," he said. "I know you are. But I just found you." He stared into her eyes, pleading. "I don't want to lose you."

"This isn't about you. Or me. It's about doing what's right." She eased from his grasp. "If the captain thinks I can help by agreeing to meet with Meredes, then I have to do it."

Instead of telling her that he didn't like it but he understood—words she wanted, even needed, to hear from him—he turned away. He retreated to the other side of the room, arms folded over his chest, expression sullen.

She struggled to compose herself, to face the others as a strong, determined woman, not letting them see her heartbreak. One night and a few kisses didn't mean Michael had a claim on her, though the pain in her chest as she thought this warned her he might have already staked out a territory she didn't want to relinquish.

Chapter Fourteen

"You hold on to that steering wheel any tighter it's going to come off in your hands. Might make driving awkward."

Carmen spoke lightly, making the words a joke, but when Michael glanced over at his coworker in the Cruiser's passenger seat, she was studying him intently. "You need to relax," she said. "An overbearing attitude isn't going to go over well with a woman like Abby."

He glanced in the mirror at the car behind him, which contained Abby and Simon, but the glare of the sun on the tinted windshield made it impossible to see into the vehicle.

"Leave her alone for a while," Carmen said. "Give her some space and she'll come around."

"What do you know about it?" he asked, annoyed. "Were you eavesdropping?"

"I didn't have to hear a word to know she was upset. Her body language when you ordered her to stand down told the whole story. She wanted you to back her up on this and instead, you tried to shut her down." She shook her head. "Wrong move."

"Shut up." He didn't need anyone telling him where he'd gone wrong with Abby. He'd known he was making a mistake as soon as the words were out of his mouth, but he couldn't stop himself from saying them. She needed someone to look out for her. She'd been pushing through on her own for so long she didn't know how to stop fighting. He'd tried to tell her he was there for her, but instead of reassuring her, he'd come across like some big bully. And he didn't know how to correct that impression now.

Instead, he was stuck watching while she remained determined to put her life on the line to deal with a man it was his job to take care of. His only hope was that something would happen between now and then to make a meeting between Abby and Meredes unnecessary.

Graham, leading the trio of vehicles, slowed for the turn onto Prentice's ranch. The big iron gate was open, allowing them to pass beneath the massive stone archway. "Smile, you're on camera," Michael said, nodding to the lens mounted on the side of the arch.

"And here's the welcoming committee," Carmen said as a Jeep blocked the road ahead. Three beefy men in desert camo, semiautomatic rifles slung across their chests, piled out.

"Armed guards?" Michael shifted the Cruiser into Park and pulled in alongside Graham's vehicle. "Who does this guy think he is?"

"Maybe one of the richest men in the country feels like he has a lot to protect," Carmen said.

"Or a lot to hide." He unsnapped his seat belt and climbed out of the Cruiser and joined the others—except Abby, who'd remained in the car, as ordered, as they gathered around Graham.

"I need you all to get back into your vehicles," the

tallest of the trio, his white-blond hair buzzed into a flattop, said.

No one moved. Michael glared at the other two guards, who took up positions at the front and passenger side of the vehicle. They kept their assault rifles pointed toward the ground, but their manner was still threatening.

"Sir, I'll have to ask you to turn around," the tallest guard said. "This is private property."

"Captain Graham Ellison, Colorado Public Lands Task Force." Graham flashed his badge and credentials. "I'm here to see Mr. Prentice on official business."

"Mr. Prentice doesn't see anyone without an appointment." The guard's expression remained impassive, his gaze fixed on Graham. The credentials might have been bubblegum cards for all he cared.

"I think he'll want to see us," Graham said. "We've discovered what appears to be illegal activity taking place on his property and we need to bring this to his attention."

A single crease formed in the middle of the guard's brow at the words *illegal activity.*

"If you call Mr. Prentice's office, they'll put you in touch with his legal team," he said.

Apparently, one lawyer wasn't enough for this guy— he needed a whole team.

"We don't need to speak to a legal team." Graham's tone grew flinty. "We need to speak with Mr. Prentice. Call him and tell him he needs to talk to us now, or the next time he sees us, we'll have a warrant for his arrest."

The threat was a bluff. While they might find a judge to issue a warrant, they were just as likely to come up against one who was friendly with Prentice. But

Graham did a good job of making the words sound like a promise. The guard hesitated. "Call him," Graham said.

The guard turned away, though the other two remained in position by the Jeep. Michael tapped his foot. If it was up to him, he'd hit the siren and drive forward, forcing the guards to jump out of the way. But maybe that was why Graham was the commander and he wasn't.

The guard finished his phone call and turned back to the car. "Mr. Prentice will spare a few minutes for you. You can follow me to the house." He pointed to Graham. "Just you. The others can stay here."

"Dance, come with me," Graham said. "The rest of you stay here."

Michael moved toward Graham's Cruiser. The guard started to argue, but Graham cut him off. "I'm not going in alone. You wouldn't."

The guard frowned, but nodded and returned to his Jeep. A quarter mile down the drive, a second Jeep fell in behind them. "These people are really beginning to annoy me," Michael said.

"That's probably the point," Graham says. "He wants to rattle us."

"I didn't say I was rattled—just annoyed." He scowled at the building that loomed in front of them. Richard Prentice's "ranch house" was a castle, complete with gray stone walls and a round tower. The three-bay garage to one side was larger than most homes.

Graham parked the Cruiser behind a black Escalade that sat in front of the door, and they climbed out and followed the guards into a dark foyer. After the bright light outside, Michael couldn't make out much about the interior of the house. A long hall seemed to lead farther into the dwelling, but the guard ushered them into a small room just off the foyer. Lined with bookshelves, this room seemed to be a library, though Michael wondered if their host had ever opened most of the matched leather-bound volumes that filled the shelves in neat, coordinated rows.

They waited a full ten minutes, Michael pacing while Graham sat quietly. Neither man said a thing. Michael was sure Prentice had the room bugged—all those books could conceal a lot of recording equipment. "He's not going to see us," Michael said finally. "I think we should go ahead and call the judge, get the warrant."

Thirty seconds later, the door to the room opened and a short man in an expensive suit strolled in. "Richard Prentice." He offered his hand. "Sorry to have kept you waiting."

Based on his reputation for outsize behavior, Michael was startled to find that the man himself was so unimpressive. The ring on his finger was probably worth more than Michael made all year, but Prentice was barely five-eight, and his hair was thinning.

"The phone call I received led me to believe you're accusing me of some illegal activity," Prentice said.

"Not at all," Graham said. "But we wanted to alert you to some illegal activity going on on your property— I know you'll want to cooperate in getting the criminals off your land and in jail where they belong."

"Won't you sit down?" Prentice indicated a pair of wing-back chairs arranged on either side of a small table. He and Graham sat, while Michael remained standing.

Prentice perched on the edge of his chair, gripping

his knees. "You'll need to explain things a little more clearly before I decide if I'm going to 'cooperate.'" He didn't exactly make quote marks in the air around the word, but Michael heard the qualifiers in his tone of voice. Prentice hadn't gotten where he was by cooperating with anyone.

"We've been investigating a possible human trafficking case on federal lands adjacent to your ranch," Graham said. "A man named Raul Meredes, with ties to a Mexican drug cartel, may be behind the ring."

Michael studied Prentice, watching for a reaction to Meredes's name. Did he imagine the way Prentice's lips compressed and the muscles of his jaw tightened? "I've never heard of him," Prentice said. "What does any of this have to do with me?"

"Our aerial reconnaissance has revealed a possible camp where we believe Meredes is holding a number of illegal aliens captive, located just outside the borders of your property."

Prentice's frown deepened at the words *aerial reconnaissance*, but he let it pass. "Let me make sure I understand you, Captain," he said. "This isn't happening on my property."

"No, but—"

"Then, it really isn't my concern." He stepped aside. "You may leave now."

Graham held up his hand. "We have reason to believe Meredes has been using the area—including portions of your estate—for the manufacture and production of narcotics, and as a way station for a human trafficking pipeline from Mexico and South America into Denver."

"Drugs and human trafficking. Those are pretty serious charges. I think I would have noticed if anything like that was taking place around here, and I can promise you, I haven't."

"Your property encompasses over five hundred acres," Graham said. "I think it would be impossible to monitor everything that takes place on an estate that size, especially when so much of it is roadless and rugged. We believe an operation that began on public lands has spilled over onto your property."

"But you don't have proof of that." He looked as calm as if he was discussing the weather.

"If the trailers we spotted from the air are part of the illegal camp, the only way they could have reached their current location is by crossing your land," Graham said.

"I don't put much stock in speculation." He stood back, a clear signal of dismissal. "Thank you for letting me know about this, gentlemen. I'll have my men investigate the matter and I'll let you know what I find."

"This isn't a matter for civilians," Graham said. "We'll need to conduct the investigation. That means we need access across your land to the site."

Prentice looked as if he'd bitten into something rotten. "I see where this is going. This was all a ruse to gain access to my property."

"The lives of innocent people are at stake here, Mr. Prentice."

"If, as you say, they're in this country illegally, and involved in the manufacture and distribution of drugs, then they are far from innocent."

Michael wondered if Prentice practiced that sneer in the mirror, or if it came naturally.

"All we're asking is permission to bring our crews and equipment across your land," Graham said. "On a road that until your court action was a public thoroughfare."

"The court has sided with me in agreeing that the road is private. And my property is private. I won't have you using it to harass me further."

"Mr. Prentice, this may be hard for you to believe, but the world does not revolve around you," Michael said. "This is about other innocent lives that are in danger. Any momentary discomfort for you is incidental."

Prentice glared at him. "I'll ask you to leave now." He turned to Graham. "If you do try anything, my private security force will prevent you from proceeding further. You'll also be hearing from my attorneys."

Graham took a step toward Prentice. He towered over the businessman by at least six inches, and outweighed him by fifty pounds. He didn't raise his voice, because he didn't have to. Years of command, first in the marines, then in law enforcement, had imbued him with a sense of authority. "You can either cooperate and give us access to the approach to that canyon, or I *will* obtain a warrant to search this property. We'll bring in dog teams and helicopters and CSI and everyone else we can think of. We'll search every inch of this place. And I'll make sure the press knows why."

Sweat beaded on Prentice's upper lip, though his expression didn't change. "That's an invasion of privacy."

"Yes, it is. But one that would be necessary."

Michael could practically hear the man's teeth grinding, but Graham had him backed into a corner, and he knew it. He might successfully stall for a while, but if Graham carried out his threat—especially if he got the media involved—Prentice would have no peace for weeks, even months. "You don't really give me any choice, do you?" he said.

"Not really," Graham answered.

Prentice stepped back. "Fine. Use the road. But my men will be watching, and if you travel too far afield, you will need that warrant."

Graham nodded. "Thank you. We appreciate your cooperation." He moved past the businessman; Michael followed.

They'd reached the front door when Prentice's voice rang out behind them. "What will you do with Meredes?" he asked.

Graham looked back. "We'll arrest him and question him. We don't believe he's acting alone. We believe he has someone in Colorado—someone with money and power—who is funding his operations. Possibly a large landowner with a history of antagonism toward the government."

Prentice's face reddened. "What are you saying?"

"I'm not saying anything, Mr. Prentice. Merely answering your question." He nodded. "Goodbye."

Michael waited until they were back in the vehicle before he spoke. "I don't trust him," he said. "He's hiding something."

"He's probably hiding a lot of things," Graham said. "Whether it's anything we're interested in or not, I don't know."

Right. What did they care about Prentice? "What next?"

"Now we see what Randall and Marco uncovered."

They returned to the others, who stood in a cluster around the two Cruisers, Abby with them. Their eyes met, hers full of questions. He resisted the urge to go to her; now wasn't the time. "We have Mr. Prentice's permission to use the road," Graham said.

"We'll escort you," the guard said.

Graham shrugged. "Do you know where we're going?"

"We'll follow you." The guard looked toward the others.

"Don't even think about suggesting they stay behind," Graham said.

They returned to their vehicles and formed a caravan, this time with the guards' two Jeeps bringing up the rear. "What happened in there?" Carmen asked as Michael guided his Cruiser behind Graham's.

"About what we expected—he pretended all of this has nothing to do with him, that his private property rights trump any other concerns. I don't trust him."

"We've never trusted him," Carmen said. "That doesn't mean he's guilty of anything. Maybe he really did close the road after noticing an uptick in traffic. He might not have anything to do with Meredes."

"Then why not cooperate with our efforts to stop him?"

"He's made his reputation out of not cooperating with the Feds on anything. What does he have to gain by doing so now? And he did cooperate in the end. How did Graham manage that?"

"He promised to come back with a warrant and a search team to tear the whole place apart. That worried Prentice enough to give in. But I'm sure we'll be hearing from his lawyers."

"And probably a few journalists. I've noticed he likes to make his case in the press, and they eat it up."

He didn't care about the press. "I wish now Abby had stayed at headquarters."

"Then you would have had to stay, too. Meredes might have decided that was the perfect time to swoop in and take her and the baby."

"You could have stayed with her." Not that staying with Abby was a hardship, but he had a job to do. Staying out of the fray when people needed help struck him as wrong.

"Uh-uh. You signed on for bodyguard duty, not me. Why would I want to sit out the action?"

"I know Spanish. A lot of these immigrants don't speak any English."

"I know Spanish, too, amigo."

They stopped at the edge of the wash. Graham climbed out of his Cruiser and the others joined him. "Randall and Marco said they think the trailers are down here," he said.

"In the bottom of the wash?" Simon looked skeptical.

Graham walked to the edge the ravine and took out a pair of binoculars. "I see something." He passed the glasses to Michael. Sunlight glinted off metal at the bottom of the wash.

One of the guards had out his own binoculars. "Looks to me as if the rancher who owned this before used it as a dump site," he said. "People did that back then—when a ravine was full of junk cars and metal, they'd haul in a load of dirt to cover it up."

"There's no rust on that metal," Michael said. "It hasn't been sitting there for decades."

Graham reached into the Cruiser for his pack. "We'd better go down there."

"We'd better hurry," Carmen said. She'd taken out her own pair of binoculars. "I see movement." She focused the glasses closer. "It's a woman, and she's waving something. I think she's signaling for help."

Chapter Fifteen

Abby stood on tiptoe, trying to see what was happening in the ravine, but here by the Cruiser, she was too far away from the action. Apparently, they'd found some people alive down there, but she had no idea who. She wanted to be helping, instead of stuck up here with this hot, heavy baby doll strapped to her torso. She was tempted to stick the doll in the back of the Cruiser and join the others at the ravine. Who would even notice? Prentice's guards ignored her, their attention focused on the action below.

Michael emerged from the trail that led into the canyon and she started toward him, eager for news. Despite the tension between them earlier, she was sure he wouldn't shut her out.

"Send every ambulance you can spare. And hurry." He spoke not to her, but into his phone, as he hurried toward her.

"What's going on?" she asked, meeting him in front of the vehicle.

"Hey. Are you okay?" He squeezed her arm and looked into her eyes.

"I'm fine. But what's happening down there?" She nodded toward the canyon. "Who's hurt?"

He released her and moved to the back of the Cruiser and began pulling out emergency gear—a first-aid kit, blankets and water. "It's pretty bad down there," he said. "Maybe a dozen wounded. Some dead." He crammed supplies into a pack as he spoke.

"But how?" Abby tried to take in this news.

"Looks as though somebody—Meredes and his men, probably—pulled the trailers up to the edge of the ravine and pushed them over—with all the people locked inside."

She stared at him, unsure she'd heard him correctly. "Is Mariposa there?" she asked, afraid to say the words.

"I haven't seen her yet, so maybe she wasn't there or she got away."

She hugged the baby closer, as if she could take some comfort from the doll. "Why do something so horrible?"

"I guess they weren't useful to the operation anymore. They were a liability, so he got rid of them."

Nausea rose in her throat. The man responsible for this was the same one who wanted Angelique. Thank God the baby was safe. "What are you going to do?"

He shouldered the pack. "We're going to go after him," he said. "We're going to make him pay for this."

"I have to meet with him," she said. "If that's the best way to draw him out, I have to do it."

He grasped her hand and gave it a gentle squeeze. "I know," he said. "I don't like it, but I understand. I'm sorry I came on so strong before. It's just… I don't want anything to happen to you."

"I'll be okay." She managed a brief smile. "I have a lot to live for."

He glanced over his shoulder at the ravine. "I'd better get back down there."

"What can I do to help?" she asked.

"Nothing right now. Stay up here. Out of the way."

When he was gone, she felt even more useless and worried. The sun beat down with searing intensity. Still cradling her fake charge, she moved into the shade, the shouts of those below drifting up to her as they worked to save the injured and dying. She felt numb, the way she'd felt in Afghanistan after encountering tragedy, the horror of the events too much to take.

She leaned against the tree and closed her eyes, willing herself not to fall apart. This wasn't about her. The others didn't need anyone else to look after right now. She had to keep it together.

Something tugged at her arm and she jerked upright, eyes wide, mouth open to scream, but a hand clamped over her lips silenced her. "Don't make any noise, señorita. While the others are busy, you will come with me." She stared into Raul Meredes's eyes, fighting panic, as he covered her face with a cloth and the world went black.

ABBY CAME TO in the backseat of a vehicle, wedged between the door and the body of a man who sat with a rifle resting across his knees. The vehicle hit a bump and her head knocked against the door. She grunted, the only sound she could make against the gag that all but choked her, and the man turned to look at her, then said something in Spanish to whoever was driving.

Her arms and shoulders ached from where one of her captors had tied her hands behind her back, and the bandanna in her mouth tasted of cotton and dust. Her captors hadn't bothered covering her eyes, though all she could see from here was the back of the seat in front of her, and the profile of the man beside her. He wore fatigues and dusty boots, and the hands that cradled the rifle were dirty, the nails bitten.

This man wasn't Meredes. She wondered if he was driving. Was there another guard in the front passenger seat? She and Michael had seen at least three other men with guns when they came to move the trailers, but for all she knew, Meredes had a dozen at his command.

She couldn't see the baby. They would have figured out quickly that it was a fake. They must have been watching, and seen that the others were preoccupied with the goings-on in the canyon. Or maybe Prentice had called Meredes to warn him of the task force's discovery. He couldn't resist the opportunity to snatch the child. Was he furious at being frustrated in his efforts to obtain the baby? Would he take that frustration out on her? A man who would callously push imprisoned people to their death in a canyon wasn't likely to have qualms about hurting a woman who had crossed him.

She wondered how long it would be before Michael and the others realized she was missing. They ought to be able to follow the trail of this vehicle over the rough terrain, but then what? If Meredes planned to use her as a hostage and bargain for the baby, she might have a chance to escape. But what if he wanted to send a different kind of message—by killing her and disposing of the body?

She shuddered and pushed the thought away. That kind of thinking would get her nowhere. In the army, she'd been trained to focus on escape and survival. If she could do the first, she knew how to do the second. She could find food and shelter in the wilderness. All she needed was an opportunity to slip away from Meredes and the man beside her.

The vehicle jerked to a stop, the brakes squealing. The guard got out, then came around to her side of the vehicle, opened the door and took hold of her bound arms and dragged her out of the car. A hot breeze buffeted her as she steadied herself, and she squinted at the surrounding landscape. They'd stopped at the edge of the canyon—Black Canyon, the one that gave the park its name. This must have been part of the gorge that wasn't in the national park, away from tourists and traffic.

She'd correctly guessed that Meredes was driving. He walked around the vehicle and stood in front of her. Though not a big man, he was tall, and wiry. He wore his sideburns long, but was clean shaven, his white shirt stiff with starch, his jeans precisely creased. It seemed odd to find a dandy here in the middle of the wilderness.

He said something in Spanish and the guard pulled a large knife from his belt. Her terror must have shown on her face. He laughed and waved the knife in front of her nose, then bent and cut the restraints from her ankles.

The passenger door of the vehicle opened and Abby received another shock to her system as Mariposa stepped out. The other woman frowned at her. What was she thinking? Was she upset that Abby hadn't brought the baby? Had she known about the plan to kill her coworkers by pushing the trailers into the ravine, or was she an unwilling pawn? What was her relationship to Meredes? Was he her lover? Her captor? Both?

The guard shoved Abby toward the edge of the canyon. Her heart hammered in her chest and she dug in her heels. Did they intend to throw her into the chasm and leave her to die, as they'd done with the workers in the trailers?

Her guard said something in Spanish and Meredes addressed her. "Follow me," he said, and indicated a narrow trail that led along the side of the canyon.

The barrel of the rifle pressed to her back told her she had no choice in the matter. She fell into step behind Mariposa, the guard behind her. Meredes led them along the canyon rim and then down into the canyon itself, the trail cut into the canyon wall. They descended about twenty feet, to a narrow ledge where someone had built a cabin. The stone-and-wood structure hugged the side of the gorge, blending perfectly with its surroundings. It would be invisible from anyone who didn't already know it was there.

Inside, the cabin was furnished simply but comfortably, with a double bed, a sofa and a table with four chairs arranged around an iron woodstove. The guard knelt before the stove and began building a fire. Despite the heat on the canyon rim, the air here in the shadowed chasm held a chill. Meredes shoved Abby into a chair. Mariposa filled a kettle from a water barrel by the door and set it on the stove to heat.

Meredes faced Abby and removed the gag. "What have you done with Angelique?" he asked.

"She's safe," Abby said. She watched Mariposa as she spoke; the woman's shoulders sagged with relief.

"You were stupid to think you could fool me," Meredes said. "Do not make that mistake again."

She said nothing, only glared at him. "Where is the child?" he asked.

"She's somewhere safe," Abby repeated. "She's in a

good home." She hoped Mariposa knew enough English to understand the words.

"She belongs here."

"Why? So you can make a slave of her the way you have these other people?"

He slapped her, a hard, stinging blow that snapped her head back and made her ears ring.

"That is not your concern." He shoved her into a chair, then settled onto the sofa. Mariposa brought him a mug; Abby caught the aroma of coffee. He sipped the drink and settled back against the cushions, a man comfortable in his home.

"Why did you murder those people?" she asked.

His expression didn't change. "What people are you accusing me of murdering?"

"The people who worked for you. The ones in the camp. You locked them in their trailers and pushed the trailers into the ravine."

Crockery rattled, and they both turned to look at Mariposa, who quickly turned away. Had she not known about the fate of her fellow immigrants? "I don't know what you're talking about," Meredes said, though his eyes told a different story. The hatred she saw there made her shiver.

"Some of them survived," she said. "The Rangers rescued them. They'll be able to identify you as the one who held them prisoner, then tried to murder them."

"They cannot identify someone who was not there," he said.

"I don't believe you," she said.

"It doesn't matter to me what you believe," he said. "Once I have the baby, you will be no use to me anymore."

"Do you think you're going to trade me for the baby?" she asked.

"Trade?" He sipped his coffee. "That is what I will let the Rangers think, but I promise you, senorita, you will never leave here alive."

MICHAEL HELPED LOAD the last stretcher into the waiting ambulance. The man strapped there had borne the rough ride up from the canyon floor in stoic silence, only occasional grunts betraying the pain from his broken leg and ribs. "You're going to be okay," Michael said in Spanish, and patted the man's shoulder. The man stared back at him, one unspoken question in his eyes—*why*?

Michael had asked himself the same question a dozen times in the past two hours. Why would someone do this to innocent people who worked for him? "If Meredes had no use for them anymore, why didn't he just turn them loose in the nearest town to make their own way back to the border or to find work elsewhere?" he asked Carmen as they headed back to his Cruiser. "Why go to so much trouble to harm them?"

"Maybe he wanted to make a point," Simon said. "To let word get around about what happened to anyone who crossed him. Fear is power to a man like that."

"Maybe he's just a psycho who gets off on hurting people," Randall said.

And this was the guy they were willingly going to let Abby face? Michael shuddered, and looked around for Abby. Just seeing her would make him feel better.

"Where's Abby?" he asked.

The others looked around. "Is she in the car?" Carmen asked.

"She's not here," Simon said from beside his Cruiser.

Heart racing, Michael ran to the clump of trees where he'd seen Abby last. He stared at the scuff marks in the dirt, not wanting to believe what he was seeing. "Randall, get Lotte over here," he said.

The young ranger looked up from adding a bottle of water to the dog's dish. "What is it?" he asked.

"Just bring her over here. Now."

"Lotte. Come."

The dog obediently trotted along beside Randall, to where Michael crouched next to the scuff marks. "Abby's gone," he said. "I think this is where they took her. She struggled. I need Lotte to help us find her." He struggled to keep his voice calm and dispassionate, though inside he wanted to scream.

"We don't need a dog to follow this trail." Simon pointed out across the desert. "The tire tracks are easy enough to see in this terrain."

Michael stood and clamped Randall on the shoulder. "Come on," he said. "Maybe we have time to catch up with them."

"Wait just a minute." Graham's command stopped them. He joined them in studying the tire tracks headed into the desert. "You can't go tearing off without a plan."

"Meredes probably isn't alone," Carmen said. "If you corner him, you put Abby in danger."

"She's already in danger," Michael said. "The man's a murderer."

"He took her alive." Graham pointed to the ground. "There's no blood. He probably plans to use her to trade for the baby."

"Which we can't give him," Carmen said.

Michael took a deep breath, struggling to control his emotions. "So we follow him, but we don't make any rash moves. We find out where he's taking Abby and scope out the situation. Then we formulate a plan to rescue her."

"All right." Graham nodded. "Carmen, you go with them. Keep me posted about whatever you find."

Michael pulled out his keys. "Come on," he said.

They piled into the Cruiser, Carmen in the front with Michael, Randall and Lotte in the back. Carmen rolled down her window and leaned out. "It should be pretty easy to follow the tracks through here," she said.

"He must have some kind of hideout," Randall said. "Either that, or he knows a shortcut back to the main road."

"Get the map from the console and tell me if you see any likely hiding places," Michael said. He hunched over the steering wheel, following the faint depressions made by the vehicle's tires across the prairie. He wanted to tear out across the empty expanse, but the rocky ground forced him to reduce his speed to scarcely above a crawl.

The stiff paper of the map crackled as Randall spread it out. "There's half a dozen side canyons branching off from the main gorge in this direction," he said. "Careful you don't drive us into one."

"Do you see any place that would make a good hideout?" Michael asked.

"Dozens of places," Randall said. "There's the canyons, old buildings left from the days when this was a ranch. And he could pull a trailer in anywhere. No roads, though, so he's probably not headed to town."

"Just keep following the tracks," Carmen said. She leaned forward, squinting out the windshield. "And keep your speed down, so you don't kick up dust. We don't want him to know we're tailing him."

"He's far enough ahead he can't see our dust," Michael said, but he forced himself to ease off the accelerator.

He guided the Cruiser along a dry creek bed, around an outcropping of rock. The remains of an old corral appeared on their left, ancient fence posts sticking up from the eroded land like broken teeth. "The map indicates some old ranch buildings around here," Randall said. "Keep an eye out for vehicles."

"I see something." Carmen grabbed his wrist and he braked to a halt. She pointed to the ruins of an old log cabin. "There's a car parked there."

He peered closer and could make out the front bumper and headlights of a vehicle. "Looks like an older Jeep," Randall said.

"Let's get out and take a look." He backed up and parked the Cruiser in the shadow of the outcropping they'd just passed, out of sight of the old Jeep. Michael looked through the gap between the boulders out on what must have been an old bunkhouse or line shack, the roof caved in, glassless windows showing grass and piñons growing up from the dirt floor. The vehicle, an older Jeep Cherokee, had been parked against the remains of a log wall, partially hidden from view.

He settled into position behind the right-hand boulder and took a pair of binoculars from the pack.

"See anything?" Randall asked.

"Just the Jeep. It wasn't one of the vehicles Abby and I saw at the camp. Maybe it's been parked there awhile. It doesn't look as though anything but coyotes have been out here for years."

"The maps designate the ruins as a historical structure," Randall said. "Part of the ranch that operated here before the park."

"Doesn't the park date back to the thirties?" Carmen asked.

"Something like that," Randall said. "Amazing how long things last in this dry air." He snapped the leash on Lotte. "She'll tell us if anyone's been here recently, and where they've gone."

Moving quickly and quietly, they shouldered day packs, and Michael picked up the assault rifle he'd removed from the gun safe at headquarters that morning. The memory of that first day Abby had walked into headquarters, when they'd been pinned down by that sniper, still burned fresh. He could still recall the feel of her body beneath his, and the fierce protectiveness he'd felt for her even then. Multiply that anxiety by twenty now.

They approached the Jeep from an angle, spreading out and putting Lotte in front. The dog remained relaxed, tail up, ears erect, nose alert. "She'd tell us if anyone was around," Randall said. "Whoever parked there is long gone."

"Not too long." Michael pressed his palm against the hood of the vehicle and felt the heat of the engine.

Carmen dropped to one knee at the front of the Jeep. "The pattern on the tires looks the same as the ones we've been following," she said.

He scrutinized the landscape around them, alert for any sign that someone was near. But he didn't have the sense that anyone was watching. A hot wind buffeted them, bringing the scents of sage and piñon. The only sounds were the scrape of their boots on rock and the occasional creak of a pack strap or the clink of the rifle stock against the pack. Whoever had driven this Jeep seemed to have disappeared.

He pulled a pair of thin latex gloves from his pocket and slipped them on, then carefully opened the driver's door. The brown cloth seats were worn, a rip in the back repaired with duct tape. The cup holder was empty, as was the center console and the glove box. No dust collected on the dash. "It looks like they wiped it clean," he said. "But we'll get someone to check for prints anyway."

He moved to the backseat. More of the same. He might have been looking at a used car for sale on a dealer's lot. He started to close the door when the glint of something on the floorboard caught his attention. He bent to get a closer look and his heart stopped beating for a moment. Carefully, he reached down and picked up the little ceramic figure of a brown-and-white rabbit.

"What have you got there?" Carmen came to stand beside him.

"It's Abby's," he said. "She was here." He folded his hand around the good-luck charm and looked at the seemingly empty prairie around them. A few hundred yards away, the ground fell away, into yet another canyon. Abby had been here, maybe only moments before. But where was she now?

Chapter Sixteen

"Please, make yourself comfortable." Raul Meredes motioned to the chair across from the sofa in the little cabin.

"I can't be comfortable with my hands tied like this," Abby said. She'd never be comfortable as long as she was held prisoner here, but she saw no sense in pointing that out to a man whose whole livelihood revolved around imprisoning people against their will.

In answer, he reached into the pocket of his neatly pressed jeans and pulled out a large knife. He pressed a button and a blade sprang out, sharp and gleaming. Abby shrank from it and he laughed, then grabbed her shoulder and turned her around.

Having her hands free again felt wonderful, then it felt awful, as blood flow returned and with it sharp pains like needles, up and down her arms. She massaged her forearms and wrists and looked at Mariposa, who had watched the exchange without a word. The other woman turned away, her attention on the kettle on the stove.

"Sit," Meredes ordered, and Abby did so, perched on the edge of the chair as if poised to run at the first opportunity. But she had nowhere to run, with the deep canyon on one side of the cabin and guards all around it. She wanted to ask what he intended to do with her—but she wasn't sure she really wanted to know the answer to that question, or that Meredes would tell her the truth.

She focused again on Mariposa. The stove made the cabin uncomfortably warm, even with the windows open. Standing next to it, Mariposa must be burning up, but she showed no signs of discomfort. She spooned instant coffee into two cups and added boiling water, then took one cup to Meredes. He smiled and caressed her hip, then pinched her bottom. Her expression never changed, though when she turned away, Abby thought she read disgust in the woman's eyes.

Mariposa brought the second cup to Abby. *"Gracias,"* Abby said. She sipped the brew to be polite, though she wasn't a fan of instant coffee; this concoction tasted particularly nasty.

"What happened to your face?"

The question startled her, both because she hadn't expected El Jefe to talk to her, and because most people—most adults anyway—were too polite to ask about her scar.

"I was injured in the war," she said.

"You should have plastic surgery to fix it," he said. "Without the scar, you would be beautiful."

Her hand tightened on the cup. She wanted to hurl the hot liquid into his face, but she wanted more to keep living, unharmed, so she simply said, "Some things can't be fixed."

"This is what happens when women try to fight," he said. "They are too sentimental to make good warriors. And they make the men around them soft."

She'd heard similar opinions from some of the men

she'd served with in the army. But the majority of her fellow soldiers had respected her and trusted her skills and training.

"Do you have other injuries from the war?" he asked.

Everyone she knew who'd fought had injuries, even though many of them weren't visible. "I don't see how it matters to you," she said.

"I was making conversation. Passing the time." He looked offended.

She sat back in the chair, determined to appear relaxed, even if she wasn't. "How long do you intend to stay here?" she asked.

"As long as necessary," he said, which was no answer at all. She was sure he was purposely trying to frustrate her, so she said nothing.

"I will offer to trade you to the Rangers for Angelique," he said after a moment.

"If Mariposa wants her baby back, she can petition the court to return her to her." Though Abby wasn't sure how the court would view an illegal immigrant who had willfully handed over her infant to a stranger.

"Why would I waste my time with courts and judges? My way is much faster, and more effective."

He sounded so sure, but she doubted the Rangers— even Michael—would hand over the child in exchange for her. "Why do you want the baby?" she asked.

He scowled. Clearly, he didn't like being on the receiving end of nosy questions. She braced herself for an angry retort. Instead, he sipped more coffee, then said, "Mariposa is sad without her. I don't like to see her sad."

Mariposa, bent over something in the sink, hunched her shoulders.

Abby looked back at Meredes. "Are you the baby's father?"

His scowl made deep lines, like gullies, on his sun-damaged face. "Does that surprise you?" he asked. "Do you think a man like me would not value a daughter? One of the things that makes something valuable is rarity. With my wife in Tamaulipas, I have four sons. But I have only one daughter. She will be a great beauty."

Of course. Beautiful women were the ones who counted. Hadn't she been hearing that all her life?

She stood. "I'll help Mariposa in the kitchen." Surely he would think that was an appropriate place for a woman.

He made no objection, so she moved to the sink and began drying the cups the other woman washed. *"Gracias,"* Mariposa whispered, her voice barely audible.

Abby had so many questions she wanted to ask: *Why are you with this man? Has he hurt you? Why did you give your baby to me?*

But Meredes's looming presence, not to mention the language barrier, prevented them from communicating with anything beyond looks.

As she stacked the dried dishes on the shelf above the counter, she looked for a knife or other weapon. But even if she found one, what good would it do? One knife was no match against Meredes and his guards. She could see one of the men out the kitchen window, pacing back and forth, weapon slung across his chest, a cigarette pinched between his lips.

Michael and the others would be looking for her. The

Jeep tracks wouldn't have been too difficult to follow across the prairie, provided they'd discovered them and linked the tracks to her disappearance. Meredes hadn't tried to cover the tracks—maybe because he'd known that once they reached the remote canyon, locating the cabin would be more difficult. A visitor had to be practically on top of the building before it was visible, and the guards would see any intruder long before he'd be aware of them.

If he planned to trade her for the baby, he'd likely arrange some kind of meeting. That would be her best opportunity to escape. Until then, she'd remain alert and bide her time.

The dishes done, Mariposa indicated that Abby should sit once more. Abby reluctantly turned to the chair across from El Jefe. Mariposa started to sit at the table, but El Jefe held out his hand to her. *"Sentarse conmigo,"* he said, and pulled her into his lap.

Abby looked away as he stroked his hand up and down Mariposa's thigh. The other woman looked miserable, but she didn't try to fight him. Maybe she'd learned doing so was futile. And maybe he was only fondling Mariposa because he sensed it made Abby uncomfortable. She assumed a disinterested expression and tried to think of some way to distract him.

"Did Richard Prentice supply this cabin?" she asked.

His hand stilled and something flickered in his eyes—was it anger, or fear? But he quickly recovered. "I do not know this Richard Prentice," he said.

"You don't know the largest landholder in the county?"

"Maybe I have heard of him, but I do not know him."

"You're practically on his land. Maybe you *are* on

his land." She tried to remember the layout of the map Michael had shown her. The park boundary must be near here.

"I am on public land. There is a great deal of public land in Colorado, free for anyone to use. So much of it is empty. No one ever visits. This suits our purposes well."

"What is your purpose here?" she asked.

His expression transformed to a sneer, but he remained silent.

"What happened to those people we saw at the campground?" she asked. "Who were they? What were they doing?"

"There were no people," he said. "No campground."

"But I saw them. There were four travel trailers and all of these people. You moved them away with trucks." *And pushed them to the bottom of a ravine.* She swallowed hard, wondering if she dared confront him again with what she knew he'd done.

His eyes met hers, and the look in them made her feel cold in spite of the summer heat. "Senorita, if you know what is good for you, you will accept that you never saw such people," he said.

"Lotte tracked Abby right to the edge of the canyon, here." Michael pointed to the place on the map on the wall of ranger headquarters. "She was there, I'm sure of it." The frustration of being so close and not being able to reach Abby gnawed at him.

"Meredes must have some kind of hideout nearby, but it's well guarded," Randall said. He rubbed his shoulder where a fragment of rock had nicked him after the guards started firing. One minute, the three of them and Lotte had been standing on the rim of the canyon, peering down. The next they'd been forced to retreat to the Cruiser. Even Michael had reluctantly agreed they needed reinforcements.

"That's almost at Prentice's boundary." Graham traced the blue line on the map that marked the edge of park lands.

"*Almost* only counts in horseshoes and hand grenades," Randall said.

"Don't tell me a man with ties to a Mexican drug cartel is hiding out that close and Prentice knows nothing about it," Michael said.

"It's what he'll say," Simon said. "And we can't prove any different."

"Then, find me some proof that links him to Meredes," Graham said.

"What do the workers we pulled from the rubble in that wash say?" Graham asked.

"Simon and I interviewed a couple of the victims at the hospital," Marco said. "But they're terrified to say much. The man they know as El Jefe promised them work—jobs paying more than they'd been told they could earn working for the farmers or ranchers in the area. When they agreed to do the work, he brought them here and made them prisoners. During the day, they worked growing marijuana. They traveled to and from the grow sites under armed guard. At night they were locked into the trailers and more guards kept watch."

"They can't tell us where the grow operation is," Simon said.

"Do you believe them?" Graham asked.

"I do," Marco said. "It's easy to get turned around out there in the wilderness, and the guards didn't take them over any recognizable roads. They moved around a lot, to avoid detection."

"What about the woman—Mariposa?" Carmen asked. "Where does she fit in all this?"

"She didn't work in the fields with the others," Marco said. "She did most of the cooking and cleaning. El Jefe singled her out. She wasn't exactly his girlfriend, but she had special privileges."

"So he might be the baby's father," Carmen said.

"We didn't ask about that," Simon said. "We were more interested in determining how the organization is structured."

"They all said they had never seen a man who looked like Richard Prentice in their camp," Marco said. "But they didn't get many visitors of any kind—just El Jefe and the guards."

"Prentice wouldn't dirty his hands mingling with the workers," Michael said.

He paced the conference room, unable to sit. Abby had been in or near that canyon, with Meredes, he was sure. She'd definitely been in that Jeep, and left the rabbit behind. Had she accidentally dropped it, or had she left it on purpose for him to find? "We need to go back there, find Meredes and rescue Abby," he said. "Go in there with everything we've got."

"We're not going to do that." If Graham shared Michael's rage toward the Mexican, he didn't show it. "We've got a potential hostage situation. We're going to approach this cautiously and minimize the risk to everyone."

"But those people are killers." Saying the word out loud made him shake.

"That's why we won't rush in."

Graham's calm only increased Michael's agitation. *Get a grip*, he told himself, and walked away, fighting to keep his composure. Everything the captain said made sense. But his emotions where Abby was concerned didn't always respond to logic.

"You got it bad, don't you?" Randall joined him in the corner of the room and spoke softly.

"I care about her."

"Just don't let it mess with your judgment."

"My judgment is fine." But even as he said the words, he wondered. By focusing on Abby, was he losing sight of the bigger picture, the reason he was doing this job in the first place? He wasn't here to protect just one woman, but to make life safer for many people—visitors to the park, the illegal immigrants who fell victim to the drug dealers' scams and the people whose lives could be ruined by the drugs they imported. So much more was at stake than his relationship to one woman.

When had she become so important to him? He couldn't identify a single moment when she'd changed from someone who'd made a strong impression on him in the past to the woman he loved. When she'd walked back into his life that afternoon at ranger headquarters he'd been impressed by her strength and bravery, touched by her compassion, and yes, physically attracted to her. All that had come together for him sometime over the past few days. They'd clicked, and last night at her trailer, he'd been sure she felt the same.

Then he'd blown it by coming on too strong.

A ringing phone shook the tense silence of the room. Carmen answered. "Public Lands Task Force."

Her expression of calm dissolved into one of agitation. "Just a minute." She held the phone out to Graham. "It's for you. Raul Meredes."

Graham took the receiver and punched the button to put the call on speakerphone. "I have something you want." Meredes's voice, heavily accented but clear and precise, filled the room. "Since you also have something I want, I think we should make a trade."

Graham said nothing, but nodded to Simon, who went to the computer and began trying to trace the call.

"Are you listening, Captain?"

"I'm listening."

"You will bring the baby to the old water tank by the old ranch corral at eight o'clock tonight. The women and I will be there, waiting."

"We can't meet that soon," Graham said. "The baby isn't close and we have to get her. We can meet you in the morning."

Michael took a step toward the captain. Was he serious about leaving Abby with a killer overnight? Randall took his arm. Michael tried to shake him off, but the younger man held tight.

"You will bring her this evening." Meredes's words were clipped—an order, not a request.

"We can't," Graham lied. "She's in Denver. Even if we chartered a private plane and left now, we couldn't get her back here by eight." The captain's gaze found and held Michael's, sending the message to keep quiet and trust him.

Michael remained tense, but he nodded to Randall, letting him know he didn't have to restrain him anymore.

"In the morning, then. 6:00 a.m."

"How do we know Abby is safe?" Graham asked. "We don't have a deal if you've harmed her."

The thought that Abby might be injured—or worse—made Michael's stomach roil. He balled his hands into fists and waited for Meredes's answer.

"If you want to see her safely, you will bring the baby to me in the morning," Meredes said.

Before Graham could reply, a woman's breathy gasp replaced the Mexican's gruff voice. "Captain, is that you?" Abby's words were high-pitched and strained.

"Yes, it's me. Abby, are you all right?"

"Do as he says, Captain," she pleaded, on the verge of tears. "Please."

With a click, the call ended, the hum of dead air filling the room.

Randall patted Michael's back. "We'll take care of him, don't worry," he said softly.

"Oh, we'll take care of him, all right," Michael said. He blinked, trying to clear his vision of the angry red haze. He straightened and nodded to Randall to show he was all right. Rage wasn't going to get Abby back.

He turned to Graham. "What's the plan?"

Chapter Seventeen

Meredes lifted the blade of the knife from Mariposa's throat and Abby let out a gasp of relief. One moment he'd been talking on the phone with Graham and the next he had jerked Mariposa to him and pressed the knife to her throat. "Tell them to do as I say or I will cut her," he'd growled.

Mariposa, eyes wide with terror, had whimpered as a trickle of blood had formed along the edge of the knife. Meredes had thrust the phone into Abby's shaking hand. "Tell them," he'd commanded.

She'd forced the words past the fear in her throat, terrified that Meredes would kill Mariposa right in front of her.

He'd brought the women with him out of the cabin and up onto the canyon's rim. He'd refused to say where they were going, but when he'd stopped only a short distance away and pulled out his phone, she'd realized he'd only been moving to where he could get a good cell signal.

He replaced the knife in the sheath on his belt and took the phone from her. "He says the baby is in Denver. Is this true?" he asked.

The last she'd heard, Angelique was with a woman

in Grand Junction. But maybe she'd been moved to put her farther from danger. Or maybe Graham was putting off Meredes to buy time. Maybe he had a plan to rescue her. "I don't know where they took her," she said. "But the offices for the state child welfare services are in Denver, so it makes sense they'd take her there."

The answer didn't seem to please him, but he said nothing more on the subject. "Come." He motioned for her to move ahead of him, then took hold of Mariposa's arm and dragged her after them. She held one hand over the cut on her neck and stared at the ground. Abby thought of dogs who cringed at their master's abuse, yet continued to follow after them. Did Mariposa seriously care about Meredes, or did she simply think she had no other choice but to try to stay in his good graces?

Inside the cabin once more, she followed Mariposa to the sink. "Let me," she said, and took a cloth and wet it under the faucet, then pressed it to the cut. Mariposa winced, then tried a wavering smile. *"Gracias,"* she whispered.

"Leave her," Meredes ordered.

Abby ignored him. He still needed to be able to show her to the Rangers when they arrived if he had any hope of retrieving the baby. As long as he thought that, he wasn't going to do her any serious harm.

"Do you want me to cut her again?" he asked. "I said, leave her."

Mariposa understood his harsh tone of voice, if not his words. She pushed Abby away from her. Reluctantly, Abby returned to the chair across from Meredes. "As a former soldier, you should understand the importance of obeying orders," he said.

"I pledged to obey my commanders in the army," she said. "I never made that kind of promise to you."

"I am more powerful than you," he said. "That is all the authority I need."

She couldn't argue with his assertion that he had power over her for the moment, but she held on to the hope that that would change. Michael and the others would come to rescue her. But she had a long night ahead of her first.

Night came early to the little cabin. The canyon walls blocked the sun and cast the dwelling in twilight in early afternoon. The shadows continued to lengthen until full darkness shrouded the hiding place. Mariposa moved to the kitchen and began taking cans and packages from the cabinet. "Can I help?" Abby asked.

Mariposa glanced at her, then at Meredes, who sat by the woodstove, cleaning his nails with the blade of the knife. He looked up when Abby stood and moved into the kitchen, but made no objection. Mariposa handed her a can of beans and an opener, and pantomimed that she should dump the contents of the can into the large pot she'd set on the stove.

While Abby opened cans, she stared out the window over the sink. She could no longer see much of the landscape, but she already knew that the window looked out into the canyon itself. If she tried to climb out it, she'd only fall to her death, hundreds of feet below. The two guards watched the front of the little house; occasionally she heard them talking in Spanish, or smelled the smoke from their cigarettes. The back of the house rested against rock. El Jefe had chosen his hideout well for its protected position.

She glanced up at the low ceiling, then quickly away.

The gunshots she'd heard earlier must have been the guards firing at the Rangers. They'd retreated for the moment, but she didn't believe they'd give up so easily. They'd wait until dark, and come in with reinforcements.

With canned vegetables and some spices, Mariposa made a soup that was more delicious than Abby would have thought possible. Though nerves stole her appetite, she forced herself to eat a little. She needed to remain strong for whatever ordeal lay ahead.

After the women washed the dishes and put them away, Mariposa went to the bed in the corner and lay down, her back to them.

"Is she all right?" Abby asked. The other woman's sudden retreat alarmed her.

"Leave her," Meredes said. "She misses the little one."

"She must have thought the baby would be safer with me than staying here with you," Abby said.

"It wasn't me she was worried about, it was Denver. She's afraid of cities."

"Denver?"

"I told her I was taking her and the baby to Denver. She should have been happy to leave this desolate place."

"What was she going to do in Denver?"

He shrugged. "Nothing difficult. I would set her up in a house there. Occasionally, she'd entertain some friends I would send to her. Nothing difficult."

Abby watched Mariposa as he spoke. Her back stiffened, then she smothered a sob. Understanding washed over her in a sickening wave as she remembered what

Michael had told her. She forced herself to look at Meredes again. "You wanted her to be a prostitute."

"It's easier work than any she'd have found if she'd stayed in Tampico. And she could have kept the baby with her."

Except Mariposa wanted more for her daughter than a life of slavery. So she'd given her away. Abby swallowed the emotions that threatened to overtake her.

"She wants the baby back now, so I told her I'd get her for her," he said.

"How thoughtful of you."

He must not have missed the sarcasm in her voice. "She'll work better if she's happy," he said.

But how could anyone kept a prisoner be happy? She had to do something to help her new friend, and to help herself in the process. But what? She returned to her seat on the sofa and tried to think, but her thoughts spun in circles. After a while, lulled by the silence and weary from the stressful day, she dozed.

"The water tank where Meredes wants to meet is here." Graham indicated the dot on the map labeled Historic Structure.

"And the Jeep was parked about here." Randall pointed to a second dot, several hundred yards from the first.

"And we were fired on from here." Marco indicated a spot on the edge of the canyon. "So the hideout is probably very near there. The shorter distance he has to travel to make the exchange, the less chance of our intercepting him or Abby making a run for it."

"Would she do that?" Carmen asked. "Make a run for it, I mean?"

Michael realized she'd addressed the question to him. "How should I know?" he said. He'd make a run for it, but Abby was a woman, and he was clearly no expert on the female sex.

"You know," Carmen said. "You've spent more time with her than anyone. Is she the type to be paralyzed by fear, or would she save herself?"

He thought back to how Abby had handled herself that first day, when they'd been trapped by the sniper. Even fighting flashbacks to the war, she'd held herself together. She'd faced her fears. And when they'd been lost in the backcountry, she hadn't panicked or blamed him, or any of the things other people might have done under similar circumstances. She'd looked after the baby, found food for them to eat and settled in to wait. "She wouldn't panic," he said. "She's the type who assesses a problem and tries to find solutions. And she'd fall back on her military training. In the army, they train you to focus on escape if you're captured, so she'll be looking for opportunities to get away from Meredes. And she'll fight back with everything she's got if she's in danger."

"That's good," Graham said. "We can count on her to help us when we get to them."

"How are we going to get to her?" Randall asked. "From what Lotte told us, they're down in the canyon."

"That's why we're going in at night," Graham said. "I'm counting on catching them unawares. And I want to take Meredes alive. We need him to tell us what he knows about the operation."

The others nodded, but Michael kept silent. He understood the importance of Meredes to the investigation, but when it came to protecting Abby, all bets were off. He hadn't saved her life once to lose her now.

ABBY WOKE WITH a start, unsure at first what had roused her, then the noise reached her ears again: a low thump, like something—or someone—landing on the roof. She stood, heart pounding. Meredes looked up from the book he'd been reading. "What is it?" he asked.

Was it possible he hadn't heard? She clutched her stomach. "I have to use the bathroom," she said. "Something in the soup didn't agree with me." Earlier in the afternoon, she'd made a trip to the outhouse perched on the edge of the canyon. A guard had waited outside the door, then escorted her back to El Jefe, who had waited for her in front of the cabin.

He frowned at her now. She bent double and moaned, loud enough to cover what she was sure was the sound of footsteps on the roof.

He went to the door and opened it, and called something in Spanish. Gunfire from in front of the cabin cut off his words as plaster rained down from the ceiling overhead. Abby looked up in time to see the blade of an ax pierce the ceiling. The ax struck again and again, then Michael dropped down through the resulting hole, landing a few feet from her.

"Are you all right?" he asked.

"I'm fine. I knew you'd come."

Meredes whirled to face him, one hand on the gun at his side. "Give it up, Meredes." Michael leveled his pistol at the Mexican. "You're surrounded. We already took care of your guards outside."

"You won't take me." Before she or Michael could react, Meredes lunged for Abby. He wrenched her to him and pressed the barrel of the pistol against her temple. "One move and I'll blow her head off," he growled.

He was as rigid as a statue, the hand clamped around her arm digging in like an iron restraint. He smelled of sweat and fear—of desperation. He pressed the gun to her head as if trying to bore a hole. She gritted her teeth against the pain and, trying to rein in her own panic, looked to Michael. His gaze burned into hers, equal parts anger, determination and caring. "Let her go, Meredes," he said. "You'll never get away from here alive if you don't."

"She'll be the one who dies if you come any closer." He moved toward the door, dragging her with him. "Call your bosses. Tell them I want a helicopter here in half an hour."

"There's no way—"

"Tell them!"

Gaze still locked to her, Michael pulled the radio from his belt. "He's got Abby," he said. "He wants a helicopter and safe passage out of here or he'll kill her."

And when he got those things, he'd kill her anyway, Abby thought. Would he push her body out of the helicopter in the United States, or wait until he was safely over the border? She had to do whatever she could to avoid getting onto that helicopter with him.

"Tell them to stand back and give me room," Meredes said.

Michael repeated the instructions. "He's coming out," he added.

Would they have had time to position a sniper in the rocks along the canyon? Abby wondered. Did they have night-vision goggles to make the shot possible?

Maybe Meredes wondered the same thing. He hugged Abby to him, his arm pressed tightly beneath her breasts, his head positioned behind hers. Even an expert would have trouble getting off a safe shot now.

Outside, the moon was a silver sliver of light amid a glittering array of stars. Dark shapes stood at a distance—other agents of the task force. "I've radioed for the helicopter." Graham's voice spoke from the darkness. "They'll be here in forty-five minutes."

Three-quarters of an hour to stand in this man's cruel embrace. Would either of them be able to endure it?

"Don't come any closer." Meredes backed away from the agents. Where was the drop-off into the canyon? She tried to remember how much room they might have, but the darkness made it difficult to orient herself. With no electric lights in the cabin and no light pollution from a nearby town, not to mention the canyon walls closing in on either side, the darkness was like a physical shroud, thick and unyielding.

"Let her go," Michael said from somewhere to their left. "Take me instead."

Meredes's laughter abraded her raw nerves like fingernails on a chalkboard. "How chivalrous of you. But you are worthless to me."

He took another step back and Abby cried out in protest. "Careful," she said. "We must be close to the canyon."

He stiffened and stretched one foot carefully behind him. Abby wondered if she could trip him, then throw herself forward, to the ground. But his grip on her was too strong. If he fell over the edge, he'd be sure to drag her with him.

"Over to the cabin," he said. "We'll wait on those rocks."

He dragged her toward the boulders piled against one corner of the cabin, then leaned against the rocks, keeping her tight against him, cradled between his legs. Her head and heart pounded in unison, a drumbeat of fear and adrenaline.

Light blinded them, a white glare that hit them full-on. "Cut it out!" Meredes shouted, enraged.

"Shut it off!" Graham ordered, and they were plunged into darkness again, blinded now, spots dancing before her eyes.

"We'll have to turn on lights to guide the helicopter in," Graham said.

"Then, wait until it arrives," Meredes said. "I still have the gun to her head, even if you can't see it." As if to emphasize his point, he dug the barrel in harder. She felt a trickle of blood run down the side of her face and flinched. He moved his free hand to cup her breast, his fingers digging in. "Just holding on tight," he murmured.

She forced herself not to react, to remain rigid in his arms. She wouldn't give him the satisfaction of knowing how afraid she was. She wouldn't let him see any weakness. He was used to people being afraid of him, of using weaker women like Mariposa. She wouldn't be another victim for him to gloat over.

Mariposa. For the first time in minutes, she thought of the other woman. Was she still asleep on the bed in the cabin? Surely she hadn't slept through this chaos. Maybe she'd followed them out and was safe with one of the Rangers, invisible in the dark. Abby hoped so. She hoped Mariposa could be reunited with her baby, and safely returned to her home, wherever that was.

Something scraped on the rock behind them, along the side of the cabin. El Jefe jerked upright. "If anyone tries anything—" he shouted. But the words died in his throat. Mariposa landed on top of them. Meredes fell to his knees and Abby kicked out against him, scrabbling away from him even as a gun exploded, deafening her. She screamed and rolled away, then Michael was pulling her up, into his arms. Light blared around them, blinding her.

"Are you okay?" Michael smoothed the hair back from her face.

"I'm fine." Her head still throbbed, and she'd have a few bruises tomorrow, but she was alive and safe. "What happened?"

"Mariposa crept up from behind and tried to stab Meredes with a kitchen knife."

She twisted around. "Is he—?"

"He's dead." Michael pulled her closer and together they watched Carmen help Mariposa from the ground and gently pry the knife from her hand. The Mexican woman was sobbing and staring at the man on the ground in front of her, blood pooling around him.

"She didn't kill him," Michael said.

Abby stared at the body of the man on the ground. "I don't understand."

"A sniper shot him." Randall joined them. "As soon as you moved out of the way, they fired. They must have been watching, waiting for a chance."

"I wondered if you'd position a sniper," she said.

"It wasn't one of ours," Randall said.

She frowned. "Then, who?"

"Someone else wanted him dead," Michael said. "Before we could question him."

Mariposa's sobbing broke the silence. The pitiful sound tore at Abby's heart. "What will happen to her?" she asked.

"We'll question her, but I doubt there will be any charges filed," Michael said. "We'll want to know whatever she can tell us about Meredes's operation. Then we'll try to find her relatives in Mexico and arrange for her and the baby to return there."

"I hope she can find a place where she can be happy and safe," she said. Wasn't that what they all wanted? She studied the man on the ground again; he looked so small and harmless in death. Yet he'd destroyed so many lives. He'd almost destroyed hers.

"I'm not sorry he's dead," Michael said. "But I'm just sorry we didn't get the chance to question him."

"You want to know who's backing him?" she asked.

"He's only one small part of the operations in the area," Michael said. "Our guess is, he was in charge of the labor force. Other people must be overseeing production and distribution."

"What about the people you found in the canyon earlier today—the workers from the camp?" she asked.

He smoothed his hand along her shoulder. "Three of them died, and some of them are seriously injured, but will probably live. We'll question them, but it's unlikely they know much. They probably never saw anyone other than Meredes and the guards. They'll be processed through ICE offices in Grand Junction and sent back home."

She looked at El Jefe's still body once more. "He got off too easy," she said.

"Forget about him." Michael gently turned her away from the dead man. "I have something that belongs to you," he said. He opened his hand to reveal the little ceramic rabbit.

Seeing the familiar token was like being reunited with an old friend; she felt a surge of relief. "I wondered what happened to it." She took it from him. "Thanks for saving it for me. I'm not sure I really believe in luck, but I like having it around."

"I thought maybe you'd left it for me to find."

"I didn't think of that." She glanced up at him. He radiated caring and concern, two emotions she'd spent a lot of time warding off, as if letting people worry about her made her somehow weaker. Michael had helped her to see things differently. Other people's compassion could make her stronger. "Besides, I knew you'd come for me."

"You did?"

"You haven't let me down yet."

He put his arm around her. "Come on. I want a paramedic to take a look at that cut on your head."

"It's nothing." She touched the tender spot and felt the blood matting in her hair.

"Humor me."

"All right. I'll let someone clean me up and slap on a bandage. Then what?"

"Then maybe we'll stop by your trailer and you can pick up a few things."

"Why do I need to do that?"

He turned her to face him and cradled the side of her face in his hand. "Because I want you to come stay with me."

"Do you think I'm still in some kind of danger?" she asked.

"No. I want us to be together."

There her heart went, racing again. So much for playing it cool and not letting him see how much this mattered to her. "For how long?"

"For as long as you like. Though forever would be fine with me."

She put her hand over his and took a step back, wanting to see him more clearly—to see all of him, not just his eyes regarding her so intently. "What are you saying?"

He swallowed. "You're going to make me spell it out, aren't you?"

"Yes."

"All right. I love you. I want to be with you. Always. I want to marry you, but if you think it's too soon for that, I'm willing to wait."

"It seems to me you've already been waiting awhile now," she said. "Five years."

"But part of that time, I didn't really know what I was waiting for."

"Neither did I." She moved into his arms once more and tilted her head up to kiss him. Here in his embrace felt like the safest place she'd ever be. As long as he held on to her, she'd be capable of anything. "I don't want to wait any longer," she said. "I don't want to waste any more time."

"Are you saying you'll marry me?"

"Now who wants everything spelled out?" She smiled. "Yes. Yes, I'll marry you. I love you and I want to be with you." Here was a man she could trust to love her, not for what she looked like, but for who she was. When a woman found that kind of gift, she'd be smart to hang on and never let go.

* * * * *

Cindi Myers's **THE RANGER BRIGADE**
miniseries continues next month.
You'll find it wherever
Harlequin Intrigue books are sold!

COMING NEXT MONTH FROM

H HARLEQUIN®

INTRIGUE

Available June 16, 2015

#1575 SURRENDERING TO THE SHERIFF
Sweetwater Ranch • by Delores Fossen
Discovering Kendall O'Neal being held at gunpoint at his ranch isn't
the homecoming sheriff Aiden Braddock expects. Kendall's captors are
demanding he destroy evidence in exchange for the Texas attorney's life...
and the life of their unborn baby.

#1576 UNDER FIRE
Brothers in Arms: Retribution • by Carol Ericson
Agent Max Duvall needs Dr. Ava Whitman's help to break free from the
brainwashing that Tempest—the covert ops agency they work for—has
subjected him to...but he's going to have to keep the agency from killing
her first.

#1577 SHELTERED
Corcoran Team: Bulletproof Bachelors • by HelenKay Dimon
Undercover agent Holt Kingston has one mission: to infiltrate a dangerous
cult. But when the compound's ruthless leader has a gorgeous former
member in his sights, single-minded Holt won't rest until Lindsey Pike is safe.

#1578 LAWMAN PROTECTION
The Ranger Brigade • by Cindi Myers
A killer is lurking in Colorado, and reporter Emma Wade is sniffing around
Captain Graham Ellison's crime scene. As much as he doesn't want a
civilian accessing his case, Graham will need to keep Emma close if he is
going to keep her alive.

#1579 LEVERAGE
Omega Sector • by Janie Crouch
Reclusive pilot Dylan Branson's mission to escort Shelby Keelan to
Omega Sector goes awry after his plane is sabotaged midair. With both
their lives in danger, Dylan no longer thinks Shelby is just a job—or that
he can let her go once it's over.

#1580 THE DETECTIVE • by Adrienne Giordano
Passion ignites when interior designer Lexi Vanderbilt teams up with
hardened homicide detective Brodey Hayward to solve a cold case
murder. But will Lexi's ambition make them both targets of a killer?

**YOU CAN FIND MORE INFORMATION ON UPCOMING HARLEQUIN® TITLES,
FREE EXCERPTS AND MORE AT WWW.HARLEQUIN.COM.**

HICNM0615

REQUEST YOUR FREE BOOKS!
2 FREE NOVELS PLUS 2 FREE GIFTS!

ⒽHARLEQUIN®

INTRIGUE

BREATHTAKING ROMANTIC SUSPENSE

YES! Please send me 2 FREE Harlequin® Intrigue novels and my 2 FREE gifts (gifts are worth about $10). After receiving them, if I don't wish to receive any more books, I can return the shipping statement marked "cancel." If I don't cancel, I will receive 6 brand-new novels every month and be billed just $4.74 per book in the U.S. or $5.49 per book in Canada. That's a savings of at least 12% off the cover price! It's quite a bargain! Shipping and handling is just 50¢ per book in the U.S. and 75¢ per book in Canada.* I understand that accepting the 2 free books and gifts places me under no obligation to buy anything. I can always return a shipment and cancel at any time. Even if I never buy another book, the two free books and gifts are mine to keep forever.

182/382 HDN GH3D

Name _____
(PLEASE PRINT)

Address _____ Apt. #

City _____ State/Prov. _____ Zip/Postal Code

Signature (if under 18, a parent or guardian must sign)

Mail to the Reader Service:
IN U.S.A.: P.O. Box 1867, Buffalo, NY 14240-1867
IN CANADA: P.O. Box 609, Fort Erie, Ontario L2A 5X3

Are you a subscriber to Harlequin® Intrigue books
and want to receive the larger-print edition?
Call 1-800-873-8635 or visit www.ReaderService.com.

* Terms and prices subject to change without notice. Prices do not include applicable taxes. Sales tax applicable in N.Y. Canadian residents will be charged applicable taxes. Offer not valid in Quebec. This offer is limited to one order per household. Not valid for current subscribers to Harlequin Intrigue books. All orders subject to credit approval. Credit or debit balances in a customer's account(s) may be offset by any other outstanding balance owed by or to the customer. Please allow 4 to 6 weeks for delivery. Offer available while quantities last.

Your Privacy—The Reader Service is committed to protecting your privacy. Our Privacy Policy is available online at www.ReaderService.com or upon request from the Reader Service.

We make a portion of our mailing list available to reputable third parties that offer products we believe may interest you. If you prefer that we not exchange your name with third parties, or if you wish to clarify or modify your communication preferences, please visit us at www.ReaderService.com/consumerchoice or write to us at Reader Service Preference Service, P.O. Box 9062, Buffalo, NY 14240-9062. Include your complete name and address.

HI15

SPECIAL EXCERPT FROM

HARLEQUIN

INTRIGUE

Navy SEAL "Rip" Cord Schafer's mission is not a one-man operation, but never in his wildest dreams did he imagine teaming up with a woman: Covert Cowboy operative Tracie Kosart.

Read on for a sneak peek at
NAVY SEAL NEWLYWED,
the newest installment from
Elle James's
COVERT COWBOYS, INC.

"How do I know you really work for Hank?"

"You don't. But has anyone else shown up and told you he's your contact?" She raised her eyebrows, the saucy expression doing funny things to his insides. "So, do you trust me, or not?"

His lips curled upward on the ends. "I'll go with not."

"Oh, come on, sweetheart." She batted her pretty green eyes and gave him a sexy smile. "What's not to trust?"

His gaze scraped over her form. "I expected a cowboy, not a…"

"Cow*girl?*" Her smile sank and she slipped into the driver's seat. Her lips firmed into a straight line. "Are you coming or not? If you're dead set on a cowboy, I'll contact Hank and tell him to send a male replacement. But then he'd have to come up with another plan."

"I'm interested in how you and Hank plan to help. Frankly, I'd rather my SEAL team had my six."

"Yeah, but you're deceased. Using your SEAL team would only alert your assassin that you aren't as dead as the navy claims you are. How long do you think you'll last once that bit of news leaks out?"

His lips pressed together. "I'd survive."

"By going undercover? Then you still won't have the backing of your team, and we're back to the original plan." She grinned. "Me."

Rip sighed. "Fine. I want to head back to Honduras and trace the weapons back to where they're coming from. What's Hank's plan?"

"For me to work with you." She pulled a large envelope from between her seat and the console and handed it across to him. "Everything we need is in that packet."

Rip riffled through the contents of the packet, glancing at a passport with his picture on it as well as a name he'd never seen. "Chuck Gideon?"

"Better get used to it."

"Speaking of names…we've already kissed and you haven't told me who you are." Rip glanced her way briefly. "Is it a secret? Do you have a shady past or are you related to someone important?"

"For this mission, I'm related to someone important." She twisted her lips and sent a crooked grin his way. "You. For the purpose of this operation, you can call me Phyllis. Phyllis Gideon. I'll be your wife."

Don't miss
NAVY SEAL NEWLYWED,
available June 2015 wherever
Harlequin® Intrigue® books and ebooks are sold

www.Harlequin.com

HARLEQUIN®

A *Romance* FOR EVERY MOOD™

JUST CAN'T GET ENOUGH?

Join our social communities
and talk to us online.

You will have access to the latest
news on upcoming titles and special
promotions, but most importantly,
you can talk to other fans about your
favorite Harlequin reads.

Harlequin.com/Community

THE WORLD IS BETTER WITH

Romance

Harlequin has everything from contemporary, passionate and heartwarming to suspenseful and inspirational stories.

Whatever your mood,
we have a romance just for you!

Connect with us to find your next great read, special offers and more.

f /HarlequinBooks

🐦 @HarlequinBooks

www.HarlequinBlog.com

www.Harlequin.com/Newsletters